BROOKLYN HARDCORE

A NOVEL

EDDIE MCNAMARA

ST ROOSTER BOOKS
2023

Praise for Brooklyn Hardcore

"*BROOKLYN HARDCORE* is a love letter to punk rock, boxing, and New York—but what's more is, McNamara throws those things into a blender and produces the kind of gritty, heartbreaking noir like they don't make anymore. An excellent, engrossing, and thoughtful read that lands every punch it throws."
- Rob Hart, *The Warehouse. The Paradox Hotel*

"*BROOKLYN HARDCORE* pops off the page as vividly as a stack of old photos from a time gone by. Snapshots that breathe and bleed with every image. As real as the scars between your knuckles, if you were there, you know. If you weren't...you're gonna learn."
-Todd Robinson, *The Hard Bounce, Rough Trade*

"*Brooklyn Hardcore* is a tour through New York's early hardcore punk scene. It reads like a thriller, and unapologetically digs into the uneasy politics of that nascent world--class, gender, race--all from practically inside the mosh pit. I loved it."
-Scott Cheshire, *High as the Horses Bridles*

"*Brooklyn Hardcore* viscerally revives a Brooklyn I'd feared was forgotten; one filled with shitkickers and zines and mixtapes. A place where the dirtbags are sometimes your heroes and the degenerates have got your back. When McNamara's characters get dealt shit hands, they make themselves a sandwich. This book is full of heart and heartbreak but make no mistake: there are no victims here. No one goes quietly into the night or cries into their pillows. *Brooklyn Hardcore* renders a world rarely given space in contemporary fiction: one where, like his unforgettable Quinny, people get knocked down and the only choice is to get the fuck back up. Bruised and battered but standing."

-Xochitil Gonzalez, NYT Bestseller *Olga Dies Dreaming*

BROOKLYN HARDCORE

By Eddie McNamara

Published by St Rooster Books 2023

Cover by Steph Murr

Contact St Rooster Books at

Holyrooster76 @ Gmail dot com

Follow @St_RoosterBooks on Twitter

CONTENTS

CHAPTER ONE: YOUTH OF TODAY

Quinny eyed the short, half-toppled fence in his backyard. A few weeks ago, his father had smashed into the structure when attempting to park his work truck in the alleyway. Defeated by the King of Beers and Detroit iron, it was now resting sideways on the thick, wild grasses and weeds around the telephone pole at the edge of the yard. Quinny got a running start and used the fence as a ramp, propelling himself upward several feet and catching hold of the cold steel spikes a lineman left in the pole.

Although he was only twelve, Quinny was already nearly six feet tall and built like a high school athlete. He pulled himself up on the pole and locked out at the top of a chin-up position. From his perch, he had an aerial view of every clothesline on Avenue P, as well as the ones on East Thirty-Third and East Thirty-Fourth streets. He spotted a thick sweatshirt on Sammy Lau's line and a heavy blanket in Frankie the Screw's yard. He let the tension in his arms slacken and slid down the splintery pole—not his best idea—before booking it over to Sammy's.

Sammy worked construction, so he left home early and wouldn't be back before two thirty p.m. No worries about running into him or his wife, who worked at the post office. Quinny grabbed the sweatshirt from the line and shoved it under his jacket.

Frankie the Screw was a prison guard and worked irregular hours. There was no telling if he'd be at the jail putting in overtime, or home trying to catch some sleep between shifts, or milling around his place, cleaning his gun. To get to the Screw's clothesline, Quinny had to hop the fence from the Lau's to the alleyway, pass five houses, and climb the gate into Frankie's yard. There was no way to do that without causing a racket due to the aluminum slats in the chain-link fence.

Quinny looked at the red and black plaid wool blanket. It had substantial weight and didn't flap in the breeze like the other garments on the line. He thought of his father, Bartley Quinn, sleeping on a freezing park bench to steel himself for his upcoming fight with the Guv'nor. It was the major underground sporting event for the winter of 1988. It would be the New York City debut for the Guv'nor, the hardest man on the London unlicensed boxing scene. Local mobsters from the Fortunato family teamed up with the London mob to fly the Guv'nor over the pond for ten bareknuckle fights. It was a hundred-thousand-dollar, winner-take-all for the fighters, and millions in action going to the gangsters.

The elder Quinn thought his shoebox-sized Brooklyn apartment was too luxurious for a properly hungry fighter. Bartley was old school, like his itinerant forebears. He looked the part, with wild blue eyes, receding red curls, and a black-tooth grin, but he needed to be as hard as granite to face the three-hundred-pound Guv'nor.

That meant toughening his spirit by sleeping rough and thickening his skin by soaking his hands and face in brine like the old-timers did. Bartley trained at the scrapyard, not a gym, and exercises included smashing tires with a sledgehammer, carrying and tossing scrap metal, and gritting his teeth through every punch that buckled the makeshift heavy bag—a duffel bag filled with sand.

Bartley spent his nights on a bench in Marine Park, a vast improvement over the prefight sleeping quarters of his youth—a mound of damp hay in a field at a Traveller campsite in the Irish Midlands. Bartley told him there were nights he was so wet and bone-cold from frost that he feared if he fell asleep, he might never wake up. Compared to that, a New York City Park bench was a luxury. The only thing Bartley had to worry about here was cops whacking the bottom of his foot with a billy club and telling him to wake up and move along. Whatever didn't kill him made him harder and more bitter.

Quinny couldn't let his dad freeze to death in the park. He kept imagining the old man being found dead on his park bench one morning. He resolved to get Bartley a blanket.

There was no delicate way to climb the fence, so he just did it as fast as possible. The aluminum made an awful sound, like cars do when they mash against each other. If Frankie was home, he'd have heard it.

Quinny landed in a crouch, sprang up, and darted to the clothesline. He plucked the first clothespin off, glancing toward the house. No signs of life. He lurched forward, ripped the second clothespin off and flung it, pulling the blanket off the line as he went. He heard something rustling behind him as he moved for the last clothespin. He felt the huge paw slap onto the scruff of his neck.

"What the fuck do you think you're doing in my yard?" The voice rumbled in his ear as he was jerked backward.

Quinny suddenly felt genuine dread. He saw himself through the correction officer's eyes. His cropped black hair, lumped-up face, and bootleg sneakers just screamed "juvenile delinquent." His very existence triggered rage in the man.

"Sir," he said, aggressively blinking and willing his eyes to well up. "I'm sorry to do this, but my family is desperate. If you could spare a blanket, I'd be grateful. There are four children who need it for sleeping. It's almost freezing out, and that's no way for a child to sleep."

"No fucking way for a kid to sleep," Frankie said. "It's pathetic, that's what it is. Your parents should be ashamed of themselves bringing children into this world when they can't take care of them. You'd be better off—"

Quinny never got to hear that gem of advice. He fixed his eyes on the corrections officer and let his vision go fuzzy. He imagined another big man in front of him—Bartley, closing in on him and slapping him with those meaty palms. He heard his old man's gruff, country brogue directing him to strike the soft spots and save his hands—a rule of thumb in bareknuckle boxing. Quinny easily parried a sloppy right from Frankie, who was nowhere near as dexterous as Bartley Quinn.

All things considered, Frankie the Screw wasn't *that* scary, he realized. Quinny flashed back to their last impromptu father-son sparring session. He'd spent the last two hours muscling a bunch of appliances out of some dude's house and decided to take a smoke break. He ducked behind a dead refrigerator in the yard with a lit cigarette and pulled his dog-eared paperback copy of *The Outsiders* out of his back pocket. That's when Quinny had suddenly seen stars.

"We Quinn men weren't put on this Earth to read books," a voice grunted. Bartley never learned how to read, nor did he think it was a valid pursuit for a real man. A calloused hand struck Quinny's left ear, and he felt searing pain followed by a loud buzzing noise. The old man had a point, he thought. What could a made-up story about a gang rumble teach you that a smack in the nose couldn't?

When Quinny looked up, Bartley was grinning wildly. Towering over his son, his freckled face was large and sweaty, the bottom half coated in a few days of orange stubble. "Defend yourself, boyo!" he said, before jabbing a steel-toed boot in Quinny's side.

After an ass-kicking that left Quinny's ears ringing and stomach churning, Bartley picked the book up, and without looking at the cover, tossed it into the nearby dumpster. Quinny never found out who won the big rumble, but he assumed it was the greasers who, he thought, were just like him and his crew.

Now, faced with this aging rent-a-cop, Quinny held back a smile at the guy's slow fists and lethargic technique. He up-jabbed Frankie's exposed throat. His dad had taught him that throat punch, a classic bareknuckle boxing move. In regular boxing, gloves protect a fighter's hands so you can fight another day. The Screw didn't expect it, so there was no way to defend against it. Who expects the neighbor's kid to punch them in the larynx? Not Frankie, who gripped his neck like he was strangling himself.

Gagging, Frankie grabbed hold of Quinny and rag-dolled him around like a shaken baby. Once he gained the advantage, however, Frankie didn't really know how to end a fight. He was used to cuffing people. Quinny grabbed Frankie's ears and bit the Screw's nose, which loosened the big man's grip and allowed Quinny to create some distance. When he had room to hook off, Quinny pounded the guard's ribs, although wasn't quite strong enough to do much damage to a grown man in that way.

Frankie got off a punch that burst Quinny's nose like a tomato. His eyes filled with tears; this time they were real. Blood and snot ran down his face in rivulets. He was hurt, and the Screw looked startled, like he just realized he'd been beating up a child.

Quinny struck Frankie's Adam's apple again, this time with a vertical fist. Frankie gurgled. Quinny threw a short left to the body, just like his dad would, pressing the punch through layers of fat. It was like reaching in and touching the man's liver.

This was another lesson Bartley had taught his son. Liver shots are worse than being KO'd the usual way when your brain rattles and the lights go out. The pain of a liver shot can temporarily paralyze you. Seconds feel like hours. It'll knock the fight out of the toughest men.

A half hour later, Quinny rolled up to Marine Park with a heavy sweater, a blanket, a broken nose, and a story for his dad.

"Good work, son," Bartley said, his calloused hands slapping the boy on the shoulder. "You never forget the first time you knock out a grown man. It's like losing your virginity, but somehow more satisfying."

Good work, son. Quinny's eyes burned for the third time that day.

CHAPTER TWO: TALES FROM THE HARD SIDE

It was four thirty a.m. and Quinny was wide awake, rage already stirring in him as he thought for the thousandth time about how he'd been betrayed by a friend. With his eyes still closed, he reached out an arm and pressed PLAY on the tape deck. The rumbling bass intro to Sick of It All's "It's Clobbering Time" helped psych him up to begin his day. When the breakdown dropped, he leapt out of bed enraged and punched a hole clear through the sheetrock wall. *Fuck!* he thought, staring at the ripped skin on his middle knuckles. It was hollow. He'd have to patch up the sheetrock before his mom noticed.

His morning ritual began with a hundred bodyweight squats. He completed these with relative ease, took a deep, restorative breath, and dropped down to max out on push-ups. At 138, his arms began to wobble. His inner voice told him to stop there, but he kept going. Each rep was slow and shaky. After counting push-up 152, Quinny was no longer able to raise himself off the linoleum floor. He stayed in that position, facedown, and took five deep, measured breaths. His heart was still pounding. He was sucking air when he turned onto his back for 250 crunches, then leapt to his feet. Out of breath, with sweat pouring down his forehead, he slipped into a pair of sweatpants and a hoodie, then laced up his Nike Air Pegs.

Quinny had to train harder than ever. He started his workouts at four thirty a.m., knowing that his former sparring partner began training at six a.m.

He walked in silence through the apartment, taking care not to wake his mother, who'd just returned from an eight-to-four graveyard shift at Store 24. His father was already up, getting ready for some early morning coaching before work. Quinny quietly walked out and checked twice to make sure the front door was locked. If he had to take a leak, he'd have to do it down the park.

He set the timer on his Casio calculator watch as he approached the track in a light jog. He bit down on his mouthpiece, an idea his father passed along to ensure he was always breathing through his nose. Mouth-breathing in a boxing match is a good way to get your jaw broken.

Picking up the pace, he held his hands high in a defensive guard and threw shadow punches as he ran laps around the one-kilometer track. *Why the fuck didn't they just make the track a mile long, like normal people?* His father told him to do eight laps around the track for his daily five-mile run.

Quinny despised running. After his first slow mile he looked at his watch and felt pure dread. There was still a half hour of hell to go, but his anger kept him moving, and his dad's words were always in the back of his mind: "Roadwork is not just conditioning for a heavyweight. Roadwork builds mental toughness.

I don't care if all 212 pounds of you hates every second out there. You press forward. If you quit on the track, you're gonna quit on me in the ring, and I don't work with fucking quitters."

Quinny slogged along until he reached the final kilometer. There, he felt a knot uncoil inside him. His body understood that the physical pain would eventually fade away, and that allowed his mind to drift for a moment. He thought about his clean-shot knockout at his last smoker fight and how it landed on the off-switch right between the chin and the ear. The kid was out before he hit the ground. But Quinny then thought about how his twenty-seventh consecutive knockout victory still didn't add up to much—he was still borrowing his father's truck and wouldn't be able to get his own car until he turned pro after the Golden Gloves. With that thought the knot in his stomach began to tighten again, and he subconsciously picked up his pace.

The main obstacle to Quinny winning the Golden Gloves was his former best friend, Tyrus Raymond. The two young men were the stars at Our Lady of Annihilation Boxing Club, the salt-and-pepper duo poised to sweep two weight classes, but Quinny had caught the rumor that Tyrus was moving up to heavyweight. He was not only going to steal the top position, but he was also going to leave Quinny with nothing. And Quinny knew Tyrus had the talent to pull it off. That was the worst fucking part.

Quinny shook himself out of it and willed his thoughts to the latest letter he'd received from

Justine Obscene, a rising star in the underground punk scene who had—amazingly—begun answering his letters.

She sent a picture this time. If he squinted and really used his imagination, she did kind of look like a crusty punk Denise Huxtable, the sexy, light-skinned older daughter from *The Cosby Show*. Posing in a short tartan skirt, ripped fishnet stockings, and platform-heeled combat boots, she was nearly six feet tall with a skinny frame and impossibly long, bronze legs. Her face was twisted into a cute scowl, her lips a slash of angry red. He could see that she had perfect coupe glass tits, and that made him think, strangely, of his mom, before she became a full-time drunk. She used to beam when his dad made her a Brandy Alexander after dinner, served in a cocktail glass he swore was modeled after Marie Antoinette's left tit.

He suddenly wanted to see Justine soften, to be the one to make her laugh and let her defenses down. That image stirred something in him so strong that he didn't care what his friends would think when he finally brought her around.

He stopped thinking once he got to the front of Our Lady of Annihilation. He opened the heavy door and took notice of the biohazard symbol freshly tattooed on the back of his left hand and the hand grenade on his right. *Cool.*

As he entered the darkened church, he dipped his fingers in holy water, blessed himself with the sign of the cross, and genuflected as he passed the altar. He opened the door to the rec center, which the local youth called The Wreck Center. He continued down the hall until he entered the cramped, overheated gym.

On autopilot, Quinny spun the combo on his locker door and opened it. He stepped into a pair of loose-fitting shorts and boxing boots. His back was to the action in the gym. His mind on Justine. As he tried to sort through his plans and longings, he forgot to wrap his hands and put on the wrong gloves—lightweight speed-bag gloves instead of properly padded sparring gloves.

Turning, Quinny surveyed the room. Father Devlin, the head trainer, and former Empire State champion, worked with Tyrus Raymond on defensive drills. Quinny walked closer to the ring, but Tyrus didn't acknowledge him. The lean, powerful young Black man focused on his footwork, shoulder rolls, and slips as he evaded the priest's punches. Not for the first time, Quinny became mesmerized watching Tyrus dodge each blow with the grace of a gymnast. With the most casual movements, Devlin's punches *just* missed every time. Then he quickly counter-punched. When Devlin mimicked a left hook, Tyrus sidestepped and fired back a simulated right cross with perfect technique.

The coaches didn't notice the way Quinny looked at Tyrus, or the way Tyrus ignored Quinny. It appeared that they didn't yet know Tyrus was moving up.

Bartley Quinn was working through two language barriers with the new kids, Dimitriy, and Edgardo. He was trying to teach them the nuance of connecting with a sneaky right hand behind the lead jab. They picked up the technique right away. *Naturals.*

Devlin's gruff voice rang out across the gym. "Jimmy Quinn in the house!"

Quinny looked over and nodded. His eyes stopped for a split second on a poster on the wall behind the ring. It featured him and Tyrus celebrating their 1993 Golden Gloves Novice Division Championships. This year, they were old enough for the open division. Everyone at Our Lady of Annihilation Boxing Club was in their corner. The hype was so real; the whole gym expected Quinny to win the heavyweight title and Tyrus to win the middleweight title. Enrollment in Devlin's boxing program went up threefold since Quinn and Raymond made the sports section.

Devlin shouted again. "Give us a show, Quinny! Murder the friggin' heavy bag, will ya? G'head. Show these kids how to put a three-hundred-pound bag out of its misery!" Devlin made the sign of the cross as a mock last rite.

Despite wearing the wrong gloves for the big bag, Quinny complied with the change of plan. He glanced to make sure Tyrus wasn't leaving, then sauntered up to the massive bag and gave it a light push with his shoulder to set it in motion. As it swung back, he dented it with powerful low hooks, letting out a grunt after each punch connected. Grown men—tough fighters—could barely move that thing, and he was leaving craters with his thudding fists.

Tyrus's ballet of violence was a compelling sight, but the entire gym stopped to watch Quinny's vulgar display of power. The technique behind his right cross was perfect: a slight step forward, a shift in the hips to generate momentum from the lower body, left glove on the chin like he was holding a telephone from the ear to the mouth, elbow pointing forward to utilize the left arm as a defensive shield, pivoting on the ball of the right foot.

When the right hand landed, it sounded like a shotgun blast. He quickly withdrew the right hand to his chin for defense as he watched the bag swing. He timed its return and smashed it with one of his monstrous left hooks. Completely devoid of proper ring technique, it was still a deadly punch. He pivoted so sharply it was as if he leapt into the punch with the full weight of his body. The bag almost bent in half; sand began to seep out where he'd cracked it open.

To summon the anger to finish the job, Quinny took his mind somewhere darker. He thought about the time he was jumped by an angry crew of Black kids on the subway. They chanted "Howard Beach" as they swarmed him. It was after a gang of Guidos chased two Black men to their deaths on the Belt Parkway. Quinny would have to take the beating for it. It didn't matter that he'd never been to Howard Beach.

He still wasn't there, so as his hands thumped, he transported himself back to age fourteen, when he lost his first three bareknuckle fights—against a laborer, a bricklayer, and the guy who held the stop sign at the construction site on Nostrand Avenue. He had to hold back tears of shame when he saw his father hand over three hundred bucks to those guys. For the Quinns, that was four, maybe five, days' worth of hauling metal—copper wiring, piping, used appliances, steel, rebar, and whatever else could be salvaged from a building before a demolition crew took over. Each day, he and his dad had to cart all that to a scrapyard, where the son of a bitch would nickel-and-dime Bartley over the haul. On a good haul, they brought home a hundred bucks. Most days, it was sixty or seventy.

He focused on the time he was having a kickaround in the front yard with his dad when half-assed wise guy Antonio "Tony Dukes" LoDuca stopped by.

"How's it been since that *titsune* bought the house next door?" Dukes asked.

"Grand," Bartley said, kicking the ball back to Jimmy. "His name is Dr. Heath. He's from Trinidad. Good man."

"You're not worried about the value of your house going down the shitter? This is the last white block left on this side of the jungle. Now that one of them moved in, they're gonna flood the place like cockroaches."

"I'm not worried about a thing," Bartley said, "I'd take ten like him over loudmouth Eye-talian as a neighbor. Can't stand the smell of garlic."

"Take it easy before you say something you regret," Tony said. "You don't have a daughter. Gotta say, your kid's got more balls than his old man when it comes to defending the neighborhood."

"How's that?"

"Who do you think's been busting this guy's windows out?"

Bartley turned to his son. "You're the one throwing rocks through Dr. Heath's windows?"

"No," Quinny said. "I never threw a rock."

"But you know who did," Bartley asked, "and you didn't stop them?"

Quinny shrugged, broke eye contact.

"Put your fucking hands up," Bartley said. "Defend yourself!"

Bartley slap-boxed the shit out of him. Quinny's ears felt like they were boiled in a pot. As soon as he slipped or blocked a slap, his father would deliver another stinging, hard slap to an undefended part of his body. Quinny was overwhelmed by Bartley's skill and aggression. *Lesson learned.*

That night, Bartley knocked on Dr. Heath's door with a six-pack of Guinness bottles in hand. Bartley aimed to make a new friend, someone to watch Manchester United matches with. Someone who agreed that Paul McGrath, the half-Nigerian, half-Irish star defender for United and the Republic of Ireland, was the best man on the pitch. When Bartley returned five minutes after he'd left, the fresh six-pack still in hand, Quinny pretended not to see his dad's humiliation. The doctor had turned the junk man away at the door.

That thought fueled three rage hooks, each thrown with more anger and determination than the previous. The bag was on its last legs when he decided to unleash the Bullhammer—the punch that his old man used to derail the Guv'nor's hype train thirty-nine seconds into his US debut, back in '88. That punch, and the fact Bartley Quinn bet everything he had on himself, bought the family a house on the redline block. That punch bought Quinn and Son Scrap Metal. That punch changed their lives.

Quinny thought about Tyrus's betrayal and hit the bag with extra fury. The sound was like a body hitting the ground from a suicide jump; the shockwaves shot up to Quinny's shoulder. Sand spurted out of the bag like water from a fountain and Quinny took a step back, gasping, watching as the bag swung and emptied its guts.

Everyone stared in wonder. Too amazed to break out a round of applause for what they just witnessed. After a moment Devlin said, "Show's over. Back to work."

Quinny tried to catch Tyrus's eye, but he was looking off into the corner. The only man in the place not watching the execution. *Afraid to face what he's got coming. Good.*

The fighters in the gym had more snap on their punches after seeing one of their teammates put on such a display. They stepped into their jabs, they remembered to use their legs, and they didn't let their hands drop.

Riding the wave, feeling the best he'd felt since he'd woken up, Quinny strode across the room to confront his former friend. Tyrus stood in the ring with his arms draped over the top rope, headgear off, mouthpiece dangling. He turned his head, finally, and looked at Quinny with a level gaze.

"Sup, Ty," Quinny said. "How about I work in with you? We can do clinch and inside game." He was showing that he didn't give a fuck.

"Nah," Tyrus said. His expression unreadable, his voice low and aggressive. "I'm gonna hit the shower. You can meet me in the cafeteria in ten minutes. We need to talk."

Tyrus obviously didn't know that Quinny knew about the move to heavyweight. So now they were going to have it out. *Good.*

The lights were out in the Catholic school cafeteria. Quinny grabbed a tray, went into the refrigerator, and snagged two chocolate milks and a cold sausage, egg, and cheese sandwich. He sat at a table in the middle of the room. The automatic lights came on, then went right off as Tyrus entered the room wearing a black and red Bally tracksuit with an Africa medallion around his neck. His hair was in a split-level Gumby cut, with the short part dyed blond. Quinny was still in his boxing gear. His mother cut his hair with the number four clip on the buzzer all around, so it looked like halfway between a skinhead and a tennis ball; he called it a Suedehead, and everyone went along with that.

Tyrus's tray was piled high with four sandwiches. Quinny took notice and tried to lighten the mood. "You didn't have to grab sandwiches for me, I'm good."

Tyrus stood, looking down at him. "You ain't good. And these ain't for you. Gotta get my weight up, you know?"

"Nope," he said, as Tyrus slid down into the cafeteria table, "I thought you were cutting weight. You're never gonna weigh in at 167 eating like that."

"Man, fuck 167," Tyrus said raising his voice. "Tell me who the super middleweight champion is."

Quinny blurted out, "Iran Barkley."

"Wrong."

"McCallum. Mike McCallum," he said with a slight stutter.

"Wrong. Try again."

Quinny stared at Tyrus and shrugged his shoulders.

"It's Steve Little. Some guy named Steve Little nobody ever heard of. Now," Tyrus said, "tell me who the heavyweight champion of the world is."

"Big . . . George . . . Foreman," Quinny said in a ring announcer's voice.

"See what I'm saying?" Tyrus said. "I gotta move up. This is real life now, no more kid's shit."

Quinny shook his head. "It's a cunt move. I thought you were better than that. Turns out, you're just another jealous bitch trying to take my shit. You know I'm gonna have to hit you for real when we do this?"

"You're not hitting anything. And it's not *your* spot," Tyrus said. "I'm putting an end to this great white hope nonsense. No Hollywood happy ending for you."

Quinny tried not to show the doubt darkening his thoughts. He felt suddenly as if he'd already lost. Size matters when boxers are of equal skill, but he knew very well that Tyrus was vastly superior in terms of ring technique.

"That's just how it's gonna be," Tyrus said. "We're fighters. We fight for the spot."

"But we never really fought," Quinny said. "We fucked around in the ring. Gonna be a different story when I'm throwing bombs for real."

"Bring the heat," Tyrus said. "You'll always be my boy, I just gotta do this for me. There are no teammates in that ring. This is what we do. And remember, you've never seen me for real either. I was playing nice with the coach's son."

The two boys stared at each other. The moment drew out. Finally, Quinny said, "When I knock your ass out in front of the whole world, remember that you asked for it. I'm going to hurt you and it's going to be personal."

"Enjoy the dream while it lasts," Tyrus said, standing up and pocketing the sandwiches.

Quinny stood at the same time. He couldn't think of a comeback, so he just straightened up, standing half in Tyrus's path, mad dogging him. Tyrus took the challenge and shoulder checked Quinny as he passed. It was barely noticeable physically, but it made Quinny see red. He grabbed Tyrus's shoulder and easily spun the smaller guy around, involuntarily readying his right hand. Tyrus reacted quickly and caught Quinny with a tap to the face. Not quite a smack or a slap, but enough to let Quinny know that he got him.

"You hit like a bitch," Quinny said.

Tyrus landed another tap as Quinny was talking. Before he knew what he was doing, Quinny had launched his whole weight onto Tyrus, grabbing his track jacket so he couldn't squirm away. He wrestled Tyrus to the ground, half under a table, and was holding him pinned.

Quinny was about to cave Tyrus's face in, just for good measure, when he became aware of men's voices saying, "Hey! Hey! What the fuck is this?" He recognized his father as one of the voices, and then Bartley Quinn's hand was on his left shoulder dragging him off Tyrus.

Tyrus looked at the men, steely-eyed, got himself to his feet, and tried to look casual as he went for the exit without looking back.

"The fuck we got here, a lovers' quarrel?" Greaser Jack said. The man's real name was Giacomo Fortunato, Quinny knew. He was a local mob boss, feared and respected like God in Quinny's circles. He stood a couple of steps behind Bartley Quinn, who still stood over his son.

Greaser Jack's hair was slicked into a perfect Elvis Presley pompadour. He wore high-waisted light-gray gabardine trousers with a banded atomic print shirt tucked in. A leather motorcycle jacket completed the ensemble. He looked like a movie star from the '50s, like Marlon Brando in *The Wild One.*

Quinny was too in awe of him to answer.

Bartley ordered his son to get off the ground and directed him to take a seat at a lunch table. The two men stepped around and settled in across from him.

Greaser Jack held Quinny under a brown-eyed glare. It looked like he plucked his eyebrows "You ever heard of a kid called Tommy Reardon?" he asked.

"Yeah, yeah, I know Tommy," Quinny said nervously. "Reardo the Weirdo. He lives near the park."

Bartley leaned in and said, "You're not to call him that ever again. Do you know about his father?"

"Uh, uh not really," he said. "I don't know exactly what happened to him."

Greaser Jack smiled and rubbed his hands together. "Relax, kid, I'm not the cops. We're just talking. I'll remember that you kept quiet, though."

Bartley interrupted, "The point is, you know that the man died from the thing nobody ever talks about."

"AIDS?" Quinny blurted.

"AIDS? The fuck you talking about? Tommy's old man had AIDS?" Greaser Jack's eyes darted between Quinny's and Bartley's faces.

"No!" Quinny said. "I just thought my dad was . . . You know? 'The thing nobody wants to talk about' and all that. I just assumed he meant AIDS."

Jack let out a deep breath, smiled wide, shook his head, and slapped the table with his open palm. "*Minchia*, Junkman, I thought I was going to have to make funeral arrangements for myself with all this talk of AIDS. Your kid. *Va fanabala.*"

So, Quinny thought, Greaser Jack was banging Tommy Reardon's hot mom. It crossed his mind that Tommy's dad might have killed himself because he was cucked by a gangster, or maybe Jack himself bumped him off.

"I need you to pay attention," Bartley said. "Jack and I are asking you to look out for the kid. He's a nervous kid; a studious, sheltered boy who just lost his father. He needs a positive male role model in his life, something like a big brother. That's you, boyo."

"Quinny," Greaser Jack said, "isn't that what everyone calls you—Quinny? Listen, we wouldn't ask if we didn't think you could handle it. I'll be around from time to time too, but this kid needs to toughen up. He's not built for this world. I need you to help him out. I see a lot of potential here. I've had my eye on you for a long time."

Then Greaser Jack did something unexpected, and slightly dramatic. He stood and began peeling off his motorcycle jacket. When he was out of it, he leaned and placed it on the table and pushed it to Quinny's side. "Pick it up, kid."

Quinny nervously grabbed the heavy old leather and lifted the garment. He turned it around and saw the back was hand-painted with the Graveyard Stompers logo: a motorcycle boot kicking a headstone, and the word "Brooklyn" underneath.

"Try it on."

Quinny stood and attempted to force himself into the jacket, but it was no use. It was at least three sizes too small for him. His arm didn't even get into the sleeve up to the elbow.

"All right, all right," Greaser Jack said, waving a hand so Quinny would stop trying to force the jacket on. "Consider this more of a symbolic offering. When I was your age, back in the '50s, I used to run with a rumble gang called the Graveyard Stompers. People always say things were different back then, but they're full of shit. Believe me, there were just as many knives and guns and drugs back then as there are now, and twice as many fistfights. The Graveyard Stompers looked out for each other. I see you and your friends. You look out for each other just like we did. I'm passing this thing on to you. I'm passing the Graveyard Stompers on to you. Look," Jack continued, grabbing Quinny's hand, "I was never blessed with a son, but if I was, I'd want him to be a tough son of a bitch like you. You'd be carrying on the tradition we started back in the '50s. Maybe you and Tommy Reardon can start the gang up again for real. You understand?"

Quinny nodded, clutching the jacket tightly in his fist. Jack said, "And do me a favor, will ya? Win the Golden Gloves for Chrissake. I'm tired of watching these shines win all the time. It would do a lot of good if a neighborhood kid won the thing. You win it and I'll take you pro. That's a promise. Don't let me down, Jimmy."

"I won't," Quinny said, trying to make sense of the situation.

"Good, good," Greaser Jack said, standing up. "I think you got a bright future. I'll be in touch with you." Quinny watched the diminutive Italian saunter across the darkened cafeteria, and then disappear through the exit door.

As soon as Jack was gone, Bartley reached across the table and seized Quinny's arm like a python around a rat. "Listen to me, son," Bartley said. "In five years, these mob guys won't be nothing but a bunch of old men in piss-stained suits. Losing their Social Security checks down the track, talking about the good old days. Do your best to look out for the Reardon kid, but don't ever get involved with Greaser Jack. Ever. He doesn't want to do you any favors—he wants to own you."

CHAPTER THREE: DON'T FORGET THE STRUGGLE, DON'T FORGET THE STREETS

Quinny and Skinhead Carlos were a menacing sight at the school bus stop. They sported shaved heads, iron cross chokers, camo pants tucked into Doc Martens boots, and shirts that read "Agnostic Front Skinhead" and "Warzone Lower East Side Crew." Their flight jackets bore the Graveyard Stompers' logo on the back, the New York Hardcore logo on the left shoulder, and a patch featuring a Trojan helmet with "S.H.A.R.P." (Skin Heads Against Racial Prejudice) on the right.

Quinny was amused at the effect they had. The moms lingering with their offspring smoked cigarettes in near silence, casting sidelong glances at the two hoodlums, and watching their kids to make sure Quinny and Carlos weren't provoked in any way. Quinny had once attended Marine Park Junior High School, but this was his first time waiting for the bus. He'd been suspended for fighting and held back so many times that he was still technically only an eighth grader. He felt absurd being there, but he had to stick around to catch the bus because Tommy Reardon would be getting on down the street.

The bus finally lumbered up, yellow and outdated, and Quinny and Carlos boarded it along with the five other youths. The driver didn't even glance at them. The two skinheads grinned ironically, stared down the kids already seated, and took a bench together in the middle of the bus. Once they were seated, the other kids began ignoring them.

Two stops later they watched intently as Tommy came up the steps and walked the aisle to take his seat. It was unbelievable. The kid wore a Poison T-shirt, ripped, acid-washed jeans, and brand-new, gleaming Air Jordan sneakers. *Sure, why not a fucking tiara*? The kids immediately began hurling insults, calling Tommy a poser, and one smartass said, “Hey, looks like we got a hot new metal chick at school!” to general laughter.

Tommy shuffled toward the back of the bus, a constipated look on his baby face, dark eyes bulging, his frail body practically twitching with nervous gerbil energy as he ran his hand through his mushroom cut brown hair and scanned for somewhere to sit. He ended up going all the way to the back, to the only open seat, which was in the zone of Nicky Baggio. Fucking hell, Quinny thought, twisting around to watch.

Quinny knew Nicky Baggio vaguely. The kid was the alpha Guido type: a chubby, swaggering loudmouth always looking for a victim. Nicky had his hair slicked back, a golden tan, and his face was twisted into a permanent menacing snarl. He wore a Champion turtleneck with a gold chain on the outside, and Z. Cavaricci pants. As expected, he took hold of Tommy's JanSport backpack as soon as the smaller boy entered their area. When Tommy tried to tug the thing back, one of Nicky's underlings stood and mushed Tommy's face with his palm and sat him down. Any fight Tommy had in him quickly drained and he simply sat, turned sideways in his seat, and watched without expression as Nicky started taking items from his bag—notebooks, pens, a textbook—and passing them around, until they got to the asshole sitting by the window, who casually tossed them out.

Quinny stood and calmly walked toward the back of the bus, steadying himself on the seatbacks as the vehicle rocked along. Carlos stood too and followed close behind. Kids nudged each other and mumbled, sensing a showdown. The space grew quiet as the two skinheads made their way. Nicky finally looked up, and his snarl slid off, and his mouth fell open until he remembered to close it. Quinny stopped when he was looming over the bully. The chatter from the other kids had completely stopped. The driver kept driving, as if school supplies weren't flying out the window of his bus as if a brawl wasn't about to kick off.

"Yo, Douche Bag-gio," Quinny said, loud enough so everyone could hear. He glared down at Nicky, who was not looking at him. "If you don't give Tommy his bag back, I'll knock out every one of your teeth, right here in front of everybody. Then I'll knock all your little friends' teeth out. Wait, I know what you're going to say—you'll go home a toothless fuck and tell your brother all about it, and he's gonna want to do something. And tomorrow, he'll come to school, and guess what? I'll knock his teeth out too."

Nicky looked straight ahead, in the general area of Quinny's crotch, not responding, probably waiting for the bus driver to intervene on his behalf. But that never happened. The driver didn't get paid enough.

"Whoever you send," Quinny continued, "right up to the poor fuck who fathered you, is gonna get his teeth knocked out, and if your mom wants some, I'll knock the mustache right off her face." This brought some nervous laughter from the onlookers.

Nicky Baggio's four lackeys remained still, watching their leader as Quinny insulted him, averting their eyes when Carlos looked at them.

Quinny bent and grabbed Nicky's book bag from the floor between the bully's ankles. "This is mine now." Quinny turned to his left. "Tommy, take your JanSport back."

Tommy leaned over and lifted the bag from the bully's unresisting hands as
Carlos turned and announced to the entire bus: "This is what happens when you fuck with Tommy Reardon."

Quinny and Carlos walked back to their seat in the middle row. Quinny ordered Tommy to remain in the seat he'd picked, making sure Tommy and the Guidos stayed uncomfortable.

When the bus stopped in front of the school, the driver pulled the lever, the door slapped open, and kids began filing off, laughing and talking about the drama they'd witnessed.

Quinny and Carlos remained seated. They watched, fascinated, as Tommy passed without looking at them, followed by Nicky and the other Guidos, whose mouths were sealed shut. Quinny and Carlos rose and followed the Guidos down the aisle. Quinny kept his eyes on the back of Tommy's head, worried the boy was going to run off somewhere as soon as his Jordans hit the pavement.

Out in the morning air, amid the flow of kids, Quinny and Carlos hustled up on either side of their man. Quinny grabbed Tommy by back of the boy's thin neck, hard, as they moved toward the school building.

"You're cutting school today, Tommy," Quinny said. "Go home and change out of this fruity little outfit, then me and Carlos are gonna show you what's up."

"Quinny," Tommy whined, squirming away from the grip on his neck. "Come on. I can't just skip the first day of school."

Carlos threw his arm around Tommy just as the boy escaped Quinny's grip. The Salvadoran's brown eyes twinkled, and his grin gleamed white. He said, "Old school, new school, true school. That's what you're learning today."

An hour later, Tommy arrived as ordered, giving a timid knock to the front door of the Quinn home. Quinny opened the door, and grimaced when he saw that Tommy was still wearing his ridiculous butt rocker outfit. "Follow me," he said, heading back to his room, where Carlos was looking through cassette tapes. As they passed through, Quinny saw his home through the other boy's eyes. The place was nearly empty, just an old couch with Mrs. Quinn passed out on it, a small TV on top of a huge, old console television, an empty bookshelf, and nothing else. No family pictures, no photos of weddings, communions, confirmations, not even news clipping from the British tabloids about Junkman Quinn's unlicensed boxing exploits, or his son's trophies and medals. Sad, bare walls.

When the bedroom door shut, Quinny pressed a plastic grocery store bag full of T-shirts into Tommy's chest. "Wear these."

Tommy crouched, set the bag down, and began pulling out the shirts that Quinny had outgrown. Most were black and faded, some were white with faint yellow sweat stains. The collars were frayed and there were small wear-holes, but that made them cooler. Quinny knew that Tommy didn't know any of the bands, but there was something like excitement in the kid's eyes as he studied the titles and logos: "Speak English or Die" with a skeleton soldier on it, "Sick of It All" featuring a New York Yankee symbol with a dragon through it, "Youth Defense League: Out for Blood," and Quinny's old favorite, a navy-blue shirt with "Judge" in yellow varsity font with crossed hammers behind it and a banner that said "New York Crew."

"Pick one and put it on," Quinny said. Tommy obeyed, stripping out of his Poison T, exposing his pale rib cage and nearly muscle-less physique. Carlos snatched the Poison T as soon as it was off and stepped over and put it in the trash basket. Tommy pulled on the Judge shirt, and as if by magic, looked less like a victim.

"Quinny, you got a pair of Dickies for this herb?" Carlos said. "We can't let him wear these booty-huggers."

Quinny sifted through a pile of dirty clothes, stood, and tossed a pair of navy-blue work pants to Carlos. "Pants off," Carlos ordered, and Tommy reluctantly began unbuttoning his acid-washed jeans. As soon as he stepped out of them, Carlos grabbed them, balled them up, and stuffed them in the garbage. Tommy quickly pulled the oversized Dickies up over his bird legs and blue-striped boxers. He had to hold the pants up with one hand until they found him a belt.

Carlos then took over Quinny's record player and acted as the DJ while Quinny sat on the bed and smiled. The blitz of the song "Out of Step" began, and Tommy got a look on his face like he was seeing his first porno mag.

"This is Minor Threat," Carlos said. "This is the first hardcore band. Your lesson starts here."

"Don't listen to him," Quinny said. "Bad Brains were the first hardcore band."

"Fuck that," Carlos said. "Nobody actually likes Bad Brains. White boys just want people to think they do because Bad Brains are their imaginary Black friend."

Quinny laughed and shrugged his shoulders. "Okay, forget Black friends. What about Black Flag?" he asked.

"Come on, yo. People just like wearing the logo," Carlos said. "Nobody cares about their music. They sold a million shirts and like ten thousand records. The first hardcore band—like really hardcore, from the streets—that's Agnostic Front. Those dudes and the Cro-Mags were robbing drug dealers on the Lower East Side with meat hooks while the Teen Idles and Minor Threat were painting their nails in art school. They're the godfathers of this thing of ours."

"No argument from me," Quinny said.

Quinny noticed Tommy trying to catch a glimpse of the tattered books in a pile near the record player. There were three Jack Dempsey biographies, *The Frontier World of Billy the Kid*, *On the Road*, and *The Outsiders*.

"Tommy," Quinny said, "do me a favor and take those books off my hands; they'll change your fucking life. Ms. Glicker gave them to me when I got expelled from school, and now their yours. You'll love them. The Outsiders were a crew just like ours, and Billy the Kid would have been one of us too if he was around today. He was born in Brooklyn, stuck up for his friends, and didn't take shit from nobody."

Tommy nodded. "You sure you want to give those away?"

"Of course, I'm sure," Quinny said. "I caught a full-fledged beating from my dad for reading during a break down the scrapyard. He says, 'You can't work and read at the same time.' Snatched the book out of my hand and tossed it right into the dumpster. Last thing I need is him coming in my room and finding those."

Tommy looked confused.

"It's cuz his pops can't read," Carlos said. "And he thinks reading makes you soft. But don't worry, it's not gonna make you any softer. You're already at rock bottom."

Quinny laughed and produced a sticker-covered Maxell cassette and tossed it to Tommy. "I made this for you. Listen to it until it's a part of you. This is the soundtrack to your life. It's the ten best New York hardcore songs ever."

He watched Tommy study the handwritten notes.

GYS Top 10 NYHC Songs

1. Outburst, "The Hardway"
2. Killing Time, "Backtrack"
3. Agnostic Front, "Victim in Pain"
4. Sheer Terror, "Here to Stay"
5. Sick of It All, "My Revenge"
6. Bold, "Running Like Thieves"
7. Madball, "Set It Off"
8. Cro-Mags, "We Gotta Know"
9. Judge, "New York Crew"
10. Gorilla Biscuits, "Things We Say"

"Put it in your pocket and don't lose it," Quinny said. "And let's get the fuck out of here."

***

They took Tommy on the D train. The kid looked genuinely scared when they hopped the turnstile at Kings Highway and East Sixteenth Street, just as the train was about to pull into the station. When they grilled him, Tommy admitted it was the first time he rode the subway to the city without his parents.

On the train, they walked between cars until they ran into the rest of the Graveyard Stompers. Tommy looked in confusion at Joe Damage, who was Korean, Cyrus, who was Middle Eastern, and Vinny Dago, who was an Italian kid with a bodybuilder's physique. Quinny could read the kid's mind and see just how shocking their crew was. Hardcore thugs from every corner of the globe. Tommy had to be wondering if this was a prank, or if they were all going to jump him once they got to the East Village.

The others had been riding since Brighton Beach. Cyrus passed an Olde English forty-ounce in a paper bag around, and they covertly drank until the train arrived at the Broadway Lafayette stop. Tommy took the bottle when it got to him, and Quinny knew it pained the kid to drink after all these guys, but after a couple of swigs, Tommy seemed to relax a little.

Cyrus bought more forties at the Optimo store, and they all moved together down the sidewalk to ReConstuction records with Tommy hanging close to Quinny, drawing from the other's confidence, starting to look like he belonged. ReConstruction was more of a collective than a record shop. They only dealt in hardcore, punk, and hip-hop. People didn't get paid to work there—they volunteered to support the scene. Tommy had some cash on him, which he'd remembered to transfer from his acid-washed jeans to the Dickies, and Quinny insisted he get Sick of It All's *Blood, Sweat, and No Tears* and the Minor Threat record with the red cover that Carlos was playing back at his house. Freddy Alva, a Queens graffiti kid who worked the counter, recommended the New Breed compilation tape he put out with Chaka from Burn. All five Graveyard Stompers agreed that was the move to make.

Quinny plucked a xeroxed flyer from the bulletin board and told Tommy they were going to take him to his first proper hardcore show back in Brooklyn that night, called the First Day of School Bash. Tommy looked half excited, and half scared to death.

Carlos led the way as they walked east to Avenue D, in search of the sketchiest bodega in Alphabet City. There were ten things sold in the whole store, and the place stank with the power of three hundred air fresheners. The windows were blacked out with posters for Colt 45.

Cyrus went to the back room for a meeting with one of the counter guys. Joe Damage brought a dusty can of Tab to the counter and tapped it four times. The counter guy went to the register, returned, and palmed something into Joe's hand. Then Joe handed him folded cash with his other hand.

Quinny smirked, watching the familiar routine. The deal was, if you brought a can of Tab to the counter, it meant you wanted tabs of acid, LSD, ecstasy, or shrooms. You got whatever they had that day. If you wanted to buy weed, you'd ask for a pack of smokes. They only had two kinds of cigarettes—Winston and Kool. Winston meant regular dirt weed and Kool was weed with a little extra—usually dipped in angel dust or embalming fluid.

A can of Coke for cocaine was a little on the nose, but these weren't the most creative thinkers. Jolt Cola got you a sack of crack. A jar of instant Café Bustelo meant crystal meth. A Heath bar was heroin. No one ever figured out what laundry detergent, Tropical Fantasy soda, or pork rinds got you. Quinny always wondered what happened when regular people tried to buy these seemingly normal items, but this wasn't the kind of place that regular people would ever walk into.

With Joe Damage tripping balls, they hopped on a mostly empty car on the train back to Brooklyn. Quinny started doing pull-ups on the handrails. Joe and Carlos started slap boxing each other and made a racket. Vinny Dago played the Backslap demo tape he just bought at ReConstruction on the big old boom box he was carrying around all day. The boys all agreed, Backslap would have been way more popular if they weren't goombahs from Mill Basin. The first track was called "False Friend" and it was hard as fuck. When the breakdown hit, Joe Damage practiced his tae kwon do jump kicks like Ray Cappo.

Cyrus went down to the other end of the train car and was scratching his graffiti tag on the window when the door between cars opened. Five Black kids with the hoods up on their Carhartts walked through, smoking cigarettes, and seeming to give no fucks.

It's on.

"What we got here?" the tallest one said. "The motherfucking Beatles?"

Nobody made a sound. The Graveyard Stompers stared at the kids in the hoodies. The kids in the hoodies stared at the Stompers.

The guy who made the Beatles comment pulled out a box cutter and dramatically pushed the razor blade out. "I don't care whose face I gotta cut to get money. Don't care if they Black or white or Chinese. I'm getting paid."

The guy scanned faces, seeing if his threat worked, and as soon as his head was turned, Vinny Dago pounced, raising his boom box. Big Vinny smashed the guy with the radio, over and over, like they were performers on Saturday morning wrestling, until the guy went down, and Vinny was able to kick the box cutter out of his hand.

With no hesitation, as if it was a practiced drill, Carlos, Quinny, and Cyrus rushed the other dudes. They squared off one-on-one. Quinny's man, it turned out, could fight. He had obviously boxed somewhere, and the two boys ended up matching skills, guards up, punches being parried, heads weaving. "I know you," the kid managed to say after he earmuff-blocked a big right from Quinny. "You the white boy Tyrus Raymond gonna fuck up in the Golden Gloves."

This pissed Quinny off, and he poured it on, overwhelmed the kid, knocked him down, and began dropping bombs. But as he raised his fist for another shot, he looked over, and saw Tommy down and bleeding, trying to get up, but unable to regain his equilibrium. Quinny jumped up, and the smallest Black kid who'd floored Tommy saw him and moved back. Before anything more could happen, somebody shouted "Five-O!" and the youths began separating but the police quickly snatched them up before they could run for it.

The cops looked like Wade Boggs, Tom Selleck, and Don Mattingly. All cops do. They made both crews sit cross-legged on the ground, then started cuffing the Black hoodie kids behind their backs.

Magnum P.I. talked to Quinny. He said they were following those kids from DeKalb Avenue. "You're the boxer, right?" the cop asked. He recognized Quinny from the paper.

"Yes sir, officer."

Quinny told the cop he was planning to take the next police officer test. That changed the cop's disposition—he went from a guy enforcing the law with a bunch of punks to a mentor advising a future coworker.

Quinny learned that trick from his father. Show you're on the side of the law. When a cop pulled his dad over for a minor infraction, Bartley would lay the brogue on thick, say how he'd once tried to become a policeman but discovered he had a heart murmur, and soon he and the patrolman were talking like old buddies. Quinny vouched for his friends and that was it. The cop shook his hand and wished him luck on the job. No cuffs. No report. No being dragged down to the precinct. "Have a nice day, officer. Be safe," Quinny said.

The Black kids in cuffs got loud when they saw that the cops were just going to let the Graveyard Stompers walk away. Quinny knew it was a shit deal, but he counted his blessings and didn't look back. *Life ain't a picnic.*

They got off the train still buzzing from the fight and walked toward the Americana Diner. Tommy was holding some pages of paper pulled out of Joe Damage's graffiti black book up to his nose. The other guys slapped him on the back and said shit happens, and at least he didn't puss out. Quinny watched, waiting for the kid to start crying or something, but Tommy was holding up. Quinny even thought he saw Tommy looking pleased with himself a couple of times. There was blood all over the logo of his New York Crew shirt, and he didn't care if heads turned when he and the Stompers went by.

When they approached the diner, Quinny got spooked. He remembered that last week, they pulled a drunken dine-and-dash on the waitress working the smoking section. She was an old lady, too old to still be on her feet all shift. Afterward, he felt bad and asked Vinny Dago, whose mom was a waitress, if that money came out of her pay. Vinny said it probably did but fuck her. Quinny thought about getting a few bucks together from the boys and hitting grandma off, making it right, but he didn't do anything. *Maybe next time.*

For now, he convinced the crew to go to a roast beef place called Zeke's. The only problem was the hardcore scene had a big overlap with vegetarianism and three of the Stompers wouldn't touch meat. When they approached the counter, Tommy lowered his bloody papers and ordered a roast beef sandwich. Carlos looked at the kid with open disgust.

"How the fuck are you going to work for world peace when you got death on your plate?" he asked.

Then Joe Damage chimed in. "Yo, Reardon, tell me the truth. Could you kill a cow with your bare hands?"

Tommy looked stunned, like he was really visualizing how difficult it would be to choke an adult cow with his bare hands. After a few seconds, he shook his head no.

"If you're not a killer," Quinny said, "you're a hypocrite for eating meat. It goes against your internal ethics. I'm gonna eat that roast beef you ordered. You haven't earned it."

Quinny saw a skeptical look in Tommy's eye, and he remembered how smart Tommy was. For just a second, he thought, *holy shit, are we all a bunch of assholes?* But then Tommy nodded and looked like everything they said made perfect sense.

Carlos ordered a french fry sandwich for himself and one for Tommy. It was just fries slathered in ketchup and processed cheese smashed down on a Kaiser roll. Tommy scarfed it down, sniffling back blood as he went, and for all Quinny could tell, it might have been the best meal of the kid's life.

"Now we're fed," Carlos said, "let's break his cherry for real."

They walked to the ironically named Crazy Country Club, a run-down old shack in the middle of some weird neighborhood near Brooklyn Chinatown. Quinny saw Tommy stiffen as they approached. They could smell weed from a block away and there were punks and skins milling around, drinking out of paper bags, and looking scary with pit bulls in the late afternoon light.

Quinny took Tommy's arm and pointed to a bunch of Brown-skinned dudes who Cyrus and Carlos had started talking to.

"Those are the Sunset Skins," Quinny said. "A Puerto Rican skinhead crew from Sunset Park. Those guys are in the middle of half of every beatdown story in the hardcore scene. Fucking living urban legends."

"They don't look like skinheads," Tommy said. The kid had red-rimmed nostrils now and dried blood stains on his shirt. He looked less like a scared loser every minute.

“Those guys are real street dudes,” Quinny said. “They don’t need a costume. When you’re like them, you can look however the fuck you want. They’re here for Merauder. A band that’s like Slayer and Agnostic Front mixed together. That dude right there is their singer, Minus. Whatever you do, don't get on his bad side.”

He pointed out a tattooed guy with a mop of hair on his head, wearing camo pants, a wifebeater, and Puerto Rican flag beads strung around his neck. Teenagers gathered around as he held court.

Quinny pointed in a different direction, and Tommy turned and saw two serious-looking guys passing out flyers. “That’s Mike Scondotto, the bass player for Confusion and Kevin McCormack from Judgment Day. They put this whole thing together. They book the shows and have a radio show at the community college that plays underground bands. There’s no Brooklyn hardcore without those two dudes. I don’t care what anybody tries to tell you.” The guys came up and Tommy accepted a flyer for an upcoming event. Reading over the kid’s shoulder, Quinny knew all the bands, or at least had heard of them: Life of Agony, Lament, Next Step Up, Patterns, Blindside, Mesk Puppies, Nobody’s Perfect, Enrage . . .

“Confusion is known as ‘Brooklyn’s Most Brutal,’” Quinny informed Tommy. “They’re the hardest band in the world. Fucking untouchable. Imagine the sickest death metal mixed with the hardest core breakdowns. You’ll see. This place is gonna go off. They got their own crew here called the Boneyard Boys. BYB ain't a real gang but they can fight. Decent blue-collar guys. The Stompers get along with them just like with the Sunset Skins."

Tommy was nodding like a teacher was describing nuclear fission to him when Carlos appeared from somewhere and said, "Let's go, herbs. Starkweather is gonna start and it's now or never if want to get up front."

Inside, the club was twenty or thirty degrees hotter than it was outside, and the place smelled like BO, weed, and hard liquor. Quinny pulled and shoved Tommy along through the crowd. Carlos stepped ahead of them, and people gave the Salvadoran a wide berth. Carlos wasn't a big guy, but he had presence and rep for sudden violence.

Tommy looked perplexed as the music started. Starkweather looked like a bunch of preppies and began their set with clean guitar and melodic vocals. "What the fuck?" he said.
Carlos leaned over and yelled, "Just wait."

Thirty seconds later, the music hit like dynamite exploding. The guitars were sludgy and distorted, accompanied by blast beats and evil growls. The club went into a frenzy. Bodies flew everywhere. People were getting pushed from one end of the pit to the other. Kids did wild dances that looked like kung fu practice. Quinny set his feet and shoved Tommy into the mosh pit. He watched the kid get bounced around like a basketball, eventually going down, so he was out of sight for a few seconds. Tommy later claimed that he slipped on a spilled beer. Quinny watched as a green-haired Asian girl took Tommy's wrist and dragged him up, and Tommy looked at her like he wanted to propose marriage, but then got clipped on the cheek by a crowd surfer's Doc Martens, and almost went down again. Quinny watched close, and when he saw Tommy shake it off and wade back in, arms and legs pumping like mosh pits were his natural environment, he knew the kid had been saved.

It was straight up *Lord of the Flies* between bands. A room full of teenage boys, half of them with messed-up home lives, hopped up on booze, drugs, testosterone, and aggressive music. *What could go wrong?* A Sunset Skin either threw a hammer or a hatchet that whizzed by Tommy's face so fast he couldn't tell which it was. It was aimed at some big doofy kid wearing a Carnivore T-shirt.

By the time Confusion hit the stage, the club was dangerously overcrowded and hot as fuck. The riffs were blistering. The bass and drums held a mosh groove, and the singer sounded demonic. The crowd was driven to violence as if they were possessed by the sounds coming from the stage. Tommy got booted in the head by a few different stage divers and pummeled it the pit.

Some newjack smashed into a pregnant Skinbird in the pit. *What the fuck was a pregnant girl doing in the pit?* Franco, the off-duty bouncer from CBGB, broke that kid's leg with a hard kick to the side of his knee. Right in the middle of the floor. More fights broke out. Four-on-one, one-on-one, everybody in the club against some drunk bikers, Carlos against anyone within three feet of him.

Quinny whispered in Tommy's ear. "There's no going back to Poison when you've seen Confusion live, right?"

"Fuck yeah, Quinny, that was insane," Tommy said.

Quinny saw Tommy's life change in the pit. He saw Tommy walk into danger and not only survive but experience the excitement and power that comes with belonging. He was one of the boys. Quinny knew that Tommy would want to stomp with the Stompers every weekend.

CHAPTER FOUR: HARD TIMES

She wasn't pretty. Any girl could be pretty. Justine Obscene was fearless. She traveled the country as a punk rock hobo, crashing on dirty floors in neglected squats, under highway overpasses, and bus stations. She documented the underground and the outsiders who populated it in her video series "ObScene." Hence the last name. She was as close to a celebrity in their world as one could be while still maintaining street cred. Quinny was obsessed with her videos. Everyone in the punk and hardcore scene worshipped at the altar of Justine Obscene.

Quinny had been nervous as fuck, pacing the floor, and his body jerked when the knock came. He opened the front door, and she was there, in the flesh. She looked exactly like he thought she would, and he felt it in his pants, all the fantasies he'd had about to be realized—he thought. But Justine just gave him a motherly hug and pulled away after the briefest embrace. In that moment he could smell her hair. Unwashed, starting to turn into dreadlocks, infused with stale smoke from clove cigarettes and sweat. No, not sweat. The smell that clings to your skin after a grimy summer day in the city. He inhaled it. He wished he could inhale all of her.

She was witchy and gaunt, with mosquito bite tits, skin the color of coffee with a drop of cream, and sharp, symmetrical features. She was pushing thirty, Quinny knew, but he didn't care. It turned him on. He stared at her gutterpunk dreads, her slender legs wrapped in ripped fishnets coming out of her tartan micro miniskirt. He tried not to look too long at her nipples lifting the front of her ratty T-shirt. She stood smiling at him, and her gold front tooth was the icing on the cake.

Quinny wished he had more to offer her. In his fantasies he would pour her a glass of wine and invite her to sit on his leather Chesterfield couch in his own Manhattan apartment. Now, in his tiny room in his parents' house in Southern Brooklyn, he realized that his version of interior design—a poster of Mike Tyson mid-uppercut and a dozen or so xeroxed CBGB matinee flyers—made him look kinda like a meathead. Problem was, gutterpunks and meathead jocks mixed like Mentos and soda, and Justine lived punk rock.

They met through a tape-trading group for extreme music. Over the years, they traded dozens of mixed tapes. She sent him anarchist punk music about dismantling the system and eating the rich, and he mocked those bands' spiky, colored mohawks and bondage gear. He sent her new school hardcore fixated on disloyal friends and scene unity, and she called it "short hair metal," "macho metal," and "music for jocks." Quinny deemed her punk rock darlings "slumming suburbanites" and "rich kid rebels." He said the only working-class person an American punk rocker knew was their parents' maid. The constant sniping, insults, and ball-breaking made their relationship fun and kept them on their toes.

After seeing a newsprint photo of Quinny and Skinhead Carlos in the underground fanzine *Maximum Rocknroll,* Justine thumbed it on the highway and rode the rails from a Berkeley punk house to Marine Park, Brooklyn. Quinny thought the article in MRR was sensationalist garbage, warning kids to beware of the Graveyard Stompers, the fascist gang who ruined New York hardcore. He couldn't understand how a ninety-nine-percent white California punk scene had the nerve to claim that his actually diverse NYHC crew was destroying punk shows, but that didn't stop them from writing it. He suspected it was because instead of being descended from West Coast hippies, a lot of NYHC kids were fuckups from group homes, the foster system, and the streets. That kind of authenticity made middle-class squatters with trust funds nervous.

Justine sat on the far corner of his bed and tooled around with her camera. The afternoon sun was bright, and she photographed him smoking a cigarette out his side window. It faced a brick wall of the house next door.

"That's the perfect image of you. It's so Brooklyn," Justine said. She spoke with a slight accent that he couldn't place. He wondered if she was a street kid or just a rich girl playing a part to get access to people like him. After all, she came all the way to Brooklyn to make a documentary about the most violent crew in the hardcore punk scene. Quinny watched Justine balance her camcorder on a milk crate to film herself tattooing "Viva" and "Hate" on his knuckles. She said it would make a great opening shot to the film. He was surprised that the tattoo didn't hurt as much as the ones on the backs of his hands. For the most part, it felt like a sunburn, and he just went along with it. Didn't even ask if she'd ever done a tattoo before.

Quinny should have asked if she was dyslexic. "Holy shit, are you sure it's not supposed to say Hate Viva?" Justine asked. He panicked at the thought, then laughed nervously before looking at his hands. Fuck. The tattoo was both backwards and awful. Still kind of badass though.

He fished a quarter-full pint of cheap Georgi vodka from under the bed and asked if she wanted a drink.

"This is all we have for two people?" she said, looking disappointed. "Maybe if we take Russian Navy shots."

Justine grabbed the bottle and poured some vodka into the cap. She used her left thumb and forefinger to open her eyelid wide. "The one useful thing I learned from the people who fucked to make me," she said, launching the shot into her eyeball, where it was absorbed with minimal spillage and no wincing. It looked like she'd done it a million times.

Quinny was not expecting to see a free sideshow act in his room, and he really wasn't prepared for audience participation. He filled the cap with great trepidation. He widened his eye, but when it came time to pour, his hand shook uncontrollably, his eye instinctively blinked, and vodka spilled down the side of his face. Justine kissed the now-watery eye and said, “You’re not missing anything. Just an instant buzz and eventual blindness.” His heart jackhammered. He chugged the remaining vodka and looked to her for approval.

She asked him to do voiceover narration. He didn’t know what to say. He felt self-conscious about his deep voice and thick Brooklyn accent. “I don’t know what you heard,” he stammered, “but the Graveyard Stompers aren’t a gang.”

“Then what are you?”

“We’re the last active crew that can trace our lineage back to the rumble gangs of the ’50s.”

“That sounds like a gang,” Justine said.

“Nah, it’s not like that. People talk about the ’70s as being hard times in NYC,” he said, “but last year there were over two thousand murders that don’t even count all the crackheads they just buried in Potters Field on Hart Island. The Graveyard Stompers are a product of our environment. There’s real violence in these streets. Somebody’s gotta have your back.”

“A lot of kids say you’re just the guys who bully the bullies,” she said.

He met her gaze and asked, “Is that a question?”

Justine shot him a glare, held her hand out, and moved her fingers in a circle, the international gesture for, “Talk, you jerk.”

Quinny grinned. "Sure. One hundred percent. We beat down the bullies. We protect our own," he said. "If you prey on the weak and my crew's around, you're gonna catch a hammer to the skull and a steel toe to the grill."

Every local scene in the country knew about them as protectors of the punks and freaks from street thugs, hoods, and Guidos. Sure, the story might have a little Robin Hood flair, but it's what they did. If you're going to make yourself an outcast, they're gonna come for you, so you had to be able to hit hard. That's what the GYS did.

"And you're the type of person who believes violence can solve everything?" she asked.

Quinny answered reluctantly. "I'm a fighter," he said. "What else do I know? Been fighting in the ring since I was four years old. It's the only thing I'm halfway decent at. I can one-shot knockout any man who breathes. I won the novice division Golden Gloves last year—crushed those kids—and I'm on my way to the open division finals this year.

"And your main competitor is Tyrus Raymond."

Quinny looked at Justine, surprised that she was aware of that situation, but he answered, "Yeah, and the fucked-up thing is, we were like brothers, me and Tyrus. Then the backstabbing scumbag moved up from middleweight to challenge me. I used to love him, but I have to kill him. Know what I mean?"

"Just to be clear, you're talking about killing a Black man. Do you understand why people feel uneasy about you saying that? About a gang of skinheads beating people down? Even if they're doing it for good, like you say?"

Quinny stayed quiet for a few seconds. This was the part he was dreading. He didn't want to say the wrong thing. He didn't want to portray his friends as the violent goons that some in the scene thought they were. "People get hung up about the skinhead thing. They don't know the history," he said. "The original skinheads in England were Black and white together. Jamaican immigrants and their working-class British neighbors dancing to ska music and shit. The average schmuck on the street doesn't know that. They only know the skinheads on *Geraldo* and *Ricky Lake*—racists and boneheads. That ain't us. We don't play that racist shit. Skinhead Carlos was born in El Salvador, Joe Damage's parents are from Korea, Cyrus grew up in Yemen, my parents are Irish Gypsies, Reardon's got a Puerto Rican mother, Lucien Pollution is Haitian, Brian 40's a Jewish kid from the Glenwood Projects. Eighty percent of the skinheads in NYC—not just our crew—are Black or Latino. But none of that shit matters. We're all straight-up New Yorkers. Don't matter where you came from, just matters how you came up."

Justine nodded, kept filming. "Was there ever a big white power presence in New York City?"

"I dunno," he mumbled. "But there's none now. Absolutely zero. We ran them all out."

"So, who are you protecting kids from?"

Quinny frowned. “Uh . . . thugs, hoods, Guidos, squares, wannabe gangsters, bullies . . . whoever crosses us. I’d say jocks, but Brooklyn’s different: jocks aren’t cool here, they have no status. It’s like, ‘go take a shower with a bunch of other dudes from the team, fruitcake.’”

Justine bit her lip to contain her smile. She hit stop on her camera, straightened and smiled so her gold tooth flashed. Quinny thought this had to be the right time. He stepped to her, put his hands on her hips, tried to move in for a kiss.

Justine kissed back, but only for a second. She tasted just like he knew she would. She leaned away and looked him in the eye. “I want you to show me something worth filming,” she said. “Take me out on the streets, show me some real Brooklyn hardcore.”

Quinny stifled annoyance, frowned again, and then got an idea. “Grab your camera and follow me,” he said. “I got something for you.”

They left the Quinn household and walked together up the street. Justine filmed exteriors as the sun was starting to get low in the sky. Quinny pointed to Nicky the Drunk and Mikey Ludes doing a hand-to-hand deal with some kid from QRB in the alleyway leading to the schoolyard. He let her know that they were coming up on Fortunato family gangsters on the next block. If she kept the camera hidden, she could get a shot of them sitting on beach chairs on the concrete in front of Big Time Party Supply. As they got closer to the park, she got great B-roll of the Midnight

Bombers Car Club, posing all juiced up in front of their Monte Carlos and Grand Nationals in the Fillmore Avenue parking lot.

"This kid we're going to see, Tommy Reardon," Quinny said, glancing down at Justine. "His pops killed himself a couple of years ago. Now there's a fucked-up scene with him and his mom. I hear that bit—I mean, that lady—I hear her screaming like a fuckin' banshee all the way over by my house. No wonder Tommy's old man did what he did."

After four blocks they stopped at a two-story red brick rectangle, which was identical to every other red brick rectangle in that corner of provincial Southern Brooklyn. Quinny stepped forward and knocked. After about a minute, the door opened, and he and Justine faced Mrs. Reardon.

The woman said, "Yeah?" then recognized Quinny and said, "Oh, hi." Mrs. Reardon was Olive Oyl-thin, with teased black hair and bright red lips that made her mouth look like it took up half of her face. She always wore ripped black jeans that were skintight with cropped shirts. When she left the house, she rounded out the look with a motorcycle jacket. She was the first, and still the most frequent, subject of Quinny's masturbatory fantasies. Five years ago, she was heavy-metal-music-video hot. She looked only a few years older than a teenager, but she had to be in her thirties since Tommy was coming up on high school.

"Mrs. Reardon," Quinny said, in a too-serious voice. "What's this I heard about Tommy's Air Jordans?"

That set her off like he knew it would. He already had the whole story from Tommy and had been thinking of how he would handle it. Now, as Justine filmed, Mrs. Reardon's eyes grew round, and she began ranting about Tommy being a little pussy, and how his father, God rest his soul, would have kicked Tommy's ass worse than the kids who robbed him in the park if he was still alive.

Tommy came out from somewhere in the house and stood behind his mother, looking sheepish and confused. When he tried to quiet her, touched her shoulder, she turned on him.

"If you want to give your stuff away, I'll empty your room myself. They can have it all!"
Quinny watched, and Justine filmed, as the small woman stormed past Tommy, toward his bedroom. She emerged seconds later, her arms heaped with baseball card binders, some toys that looked ridiculous for a kid Tommy's age to own, and a few video game cartridges.

Quinny stared as the woman stepped to the door and pitched the stuff out so it spread across the sidewalk. He had to step back to avoid being hit with an Iron Sheik figure. Justine kept her eye to the camera. Tommy was saying, "Hey, Mom! Don't!"

As Mrs. Reardon turned to go back and get more of Tommy's stuff, Quinny jumped up the step, over the threshold into the house, and took hold of her elbow.

"Don't touch me!" she said, but he tightened his grip, kept her from rushing into Tommy's room again.

Tommy was out on the sidewalk, collecting his belongings.

"Listen! Mrs. Reardon!" Quinny insisted, suppressing laughter. "I'm gonna get Tommy's Jordans back. You have my word."

"How are you going to do that? Magic? Three days' pay for those fucking shoes, and he just handed them over!"

Quinny kept his grip on her elbow and moved close to her. Their noses almost touched. Her eyes now looked uncertain. He could feel her breath on his face as he spoke softly and steadily. "Trust me. Your boy's gonna get his shoes back and this kind of thing won't happen again. I got you."

Without warning, she burst into tears and flung herself uncomfortably over his shoulder in something between a collapse and an embrace. It made his heart pound. He got a twinge of aroused nausea for the second time in the space of a few minutes. *Women.*

"Look, I'm trying my best." Mrs. Reardon sobbed onto his shoulder. "But a boy needs a father. He needs to see how a man handles his business. This kid's a genius. You know that, right? He's the top ranked chess player in the city in his age group. He got into Stuyvesant and

Dalton. But he's too soft. I can't raise him right on my own."

She lowered her voice, placed a hand on Quinny's chest, and whispered, "I know who you are and I'm . . ." She looked up, locking eyes with him. ". . . so grateful for what you're doing for Tommy."

Jesus, Quinny thought, standing there rock hard like a jackass, saying nothing for what felt like the longest time. Then he abruptly broke his gaze with Mrs. Reardon's and spoke over his shoulder, "Tommy, put your shit back in your room and come over to my place. We're getting your sneakers back."

***

The first thing Quinny did when he they got to his place was phone Skinhead Carlos. Then he took Justine back to his bedroom, looking around and thinking. "It's a go," he said while making the sign of the cross. "I'm baptizing you a Stomper, Miss Justine. Keep the camera rolling and get everything. Make sure you're ready to move when we set it off. Hide your ID. Take off any grabbable piercings. Tie your shoes tight and tuck your laces. We're going shopping for sneakers in Marine Park."

Justine kept the camera on Quinny as he sat on the bed and tightened the laces on his twelve-hole, oxblood Doc Martens steel-toe boots. Then he stood self-consciously, glancing her way, and pulled on his Graveyard Stompers flight jacket.

She followed him back out of the house, around to the backyard, where he spun the combination lock and took the chain off a light blue GT Pro Performer BMX bike. Then she followed him as he rolled the bike to the front of the house. When they got there, Tommy was waiting, glancing up and down the street, trying to put up a tough front.

Quinny tried not to think about the camera on him as he spoke to Tommy. "We're going down the park," he told the kid. "You and this bike are bait. Carlos and I get to play knockout on some motherfuckers and grab *their* shoes. If we catch the right ones, we might get yours back. If not, we'll at least get you something. You reel in enough of these scumbags, you might walk away with a free bike."

Tommy nodded. He actually looked like he might start crying, but Quinny pretended not to notice.

As they walked to the park, Justine held the camera at chest level, aimed at Quinny. "Tell me about your friend Carlos," she said.

Quinny frowned and glanced at her. "Carlos? I think that guy might just be in all this for thc brawling. I guess he got fucked up in thc head as a kid in El Salvador. He says the national sport over there is hacking people up with a machete. I don't think he's joking. Dude didn't used to know the difference between, like, real violence in the streets and the symbolic violence of a mosh pit. He would go to shows, get bumped, and crack people who were just trying to dance. Used to be banned from every club in the city. The thing is, he isn't even a great fighter. He's just up for it, anytime, anywhere."

Quinny thought a moment, and added, "But that's how it works. The average asshole, his nerves get him every time. A fight starts, he's too scared to think straight and he gets dropped. Don't matter how much time he spent at the gym or in karate class. You get a guy like Carlos—or like me—who can see what's happening, you basically got it in the bag. Like my dad says: He'd bet his house on me and Carlos against a dozen strip-mall ninjas any day of the week."

Skinhead Carlos was waiting for them when they arrived at Marine Park. True to form, the Salvadoran was eager to get to the action. He asked if the kids they were looking for were gang bangers. Tommy swore they were just two regular Black kids and a fat white kid. No tattoos, no colors.

"Here's how it's gonna go," Quinny said. "You pedal that bike around the park nice and slow, like a pussy. I know you don't have to try too hard for that, but you gotta sell it: be a scared mark out there. They can smell it."

He looked at Justine and laughingly said, "See, I didn't say 'like a little bitch.' Your Riot Grrrl shit must be making a difference. I sound like a PC punk now."

Justine rolled her eyes.

Grinning, seeing the fear in Tommy's eyes, Carlos put his hand on the kid's shoulder and gave it a hard squeeze. "It'll be easy. Go nice and slow until they see you. Let them chase after you a little, then book it over to the field house and make sure they follow. We'll be waiting behind the building—you won't be able to see us—but trust me, we'll be there for your first real Graveyard Stomper boot party. If you do the right thing, I'll baptize you one of us. Don't fuck this up, kid."

Tommy nodded, swallowed visibly, and turned to look forward. He pushed off and began pedaling toward the Avenue U parking lot. Quinny saw the bike wobble a little, but the kid was doing what he was told. Maybe he'd end up a Stomper after all.

***

Tommy cycled past the tree in front of the junior high schoolyard where his father was found hanging. He was almost surprised when he heard a voice call out. He didn't know it would be this easy to lure in predators.

"Yo shorty, yo shorty," the voice said, let me see your bike." Tommy glanced and locked eyes with a tall skinny Black kid, maybe sixteen or seventeen, standing on the back pegs of a bike that was quickly catching up with him. The kid's hands were on the shoulders of a toothpick-thin white kid, who was pedaling away, looking at Tommy with excitement. They weren't the kids who stole Tommy's Air Jordans, but Tommy knew that didn't matter.

"We only got one bike," the white kid who was pedaling said. "My boy wants to buy a bike like yours. He just wants to try it out first."

Tommy looked straight ahead and kept pedaling. He knew he looked terrified because he was. He was sure these kids were going to fuck him up before he could get back to Quinny and Carlos.

"Hey!" the white kid said, loudly. "Stop. My friend's just gonna ride your bike for a minute to see if he likes it. You can hold my bike if you want."

Tommy pedaled faster. He threw a glance behind him and saw the Black kid suddenly jump off the pegs and start running. Tommy felt a hand graze his back as he stood and began cranking the pedals for all he was worth. He heard the white kid say, "Get on! Get on!" as he braked and let the Black kid jump back on the pegs. He knew they were coming behind him, rider and passenger, picking up speed, enjoying the chase. He knew that if he slowed down or wiped out that was it.

Quinny and Carlos took their position behind the field house. Justine stood off to the side, filming it all.

The sound of a BMX bike hitting the brakes hard on a patch of dirt was the signal that Tommy was back, and it was about to kick off. Quinny and Carlos smiled with pride for that little herb. Tommy did the business.

The white kid pedaling behind Tommy suddenly hit his brakes. His eyes opened wide, and he made a *holy shit* face as he saw what was waiting for him. A split second later, Carlos smashed him with the handle-end of the Hammer of Justice—a metal claw hammer that he carried everywhere he went—knocking the kid, his bike, and his passenger to the ground. Carlos gave him a soccer kick to the crotch, then stomped on the bike that had landed on the kid's right leg. He kept stomping until the leg bent in a way legs shouldn't bend.

Vicious.

Tommy looked nauseated.

Quinny moved up and nailed the Black kid with an overhand right. The kid went down, and immediately tried to get up but slumped back to the ground and stayed that way. Quinny swelled up with pride at his one-shot KO and forced himself not to look and see what Justine thought of it.

Carlos rifled their victims' pockets and bookbags while Quinny tore off their sneakers. As the two would-be robbers began to moan and try to get up, Carlos grabbed the kid's tricked-out bike and began riding it out of the park. Tommy followed on the BMX, and Justine and Quinny began trotting behind.

Back in Quinny's bedroom, all of them sweating and buzzing with adrenaline, they divided the spoils. The take was $17.25 in cash, two fake leather bookbags, a Mongoose Expert bike, two bus passes, one gold chain, one pair of

Nike Air Diamond Turfs, one pair of off brand "reject" sneakers, one Swatch watch, one Tekken PlayStation video game, one folded *WWF* magazine, two sets of house keys, two kitchen knives, and one box cutter.

Quinny threw the sneakers at Tommy. "These are better than Jordans. Deion Sanders wears them. Hope they fit. Hey—make sure to tell your mother."

Tommy clutched the sneakers like they were a life preserver ring.

"Yo bitch, break the fuck out," Carlos shouted.

Justine didn't roll her eyes this time. She hit stop on the camera and grinned. "That was sick!" she said, her eyes wide, her gold tooth gleaming as she grinned. "This is going to be my best video ever. The Graveyard Stompers are going to be legends. And we haven't even punched any Nazis yet. You guys! I can't wait to hit up a hardcore show with the whole crew."

CHAPTER FIVE: SET IT OFF!

The Golden Gloves Open Division finals, held every year at Madison Square Garden, crowned the best amateur boxers in the city.

Quinny heard his name being announced ringside. “Weighing in at a fit and ready 212 pounds, representing Our Lady of Annihilation Boxing Club in Brooklyn New York . . . *Jimmeeeeeeee Quinnnnnnn.*” But he found himself seated on a folding chair in the dressing room, unable to move his body.

His shallow breaths made him lightheaded, confused. His legs felt heavier than marble pillars. His hands tingled under the wraps and boxing gloves. He had an overwhelming urge to get the fuck out of there. *I gotta bail on the Garden and jump on the subway back home.* Bartley Quinn knew they had a three-minute grace period, so he was being patient and psyching Quinny up. The officials would understand. It happens a lot with young boxers—they get nervous and come out late.

“What you’re feeling is normal,” Bartley said to his son, as he lifted the young man’s gloves up. “You know why they say a guy ‘beat the shit’ out of another one? Because civilians shit their pants all the time when they get hit. If you’re not comfortable fighting, the adrenaline and nerves make your body believe it’s in real danger, like being attacked by a lion. They shit their pants. You can't fight if you need to shit, so that's the body's way of helping you get ready for battle. It's just nature. But it's not your nature. You're not a civilian. You're a born and bred fighter."

Quinny said nothing, but he started to worry about shitting his pants in front of a packed arena and television audience. His mind was racing out of control. He was going to embarrass himself in front of everyone he knew and a whole fuck-ton of people he didn't know. He still couldn't move, as trapped as that mosquito embedded in amber from *Jurassic Park*.

"Before my fight with the Guv'nor, all I could think of was getting out of there," Bartley said. "I knew I was brought in to lose. I didn't want to look like a jackass and let the family down. No one gave me a chance in a million. But fuck them and fuck fear. I let it power me. Your fear is rocket fuel."

An official from the New York State Athletic Commission burst into the dressing room. He was tall and overweight, wearing a white shirt and a black tie. He ignored Quinny and looked Bartley in the eye. His voice was tense. "If your boxer doesn't make his ring walk right this instant, he loses via forfeit."

Quinny watched the man withdraw, leaving the door ajar. Quinny didn't care. He'd rather lose by forfeit than get demolished in front of his home crowd.

Then he saw stars, and realized that Bartley had whipped a big, calloused hand right across his left cheek. The sound of the slap rang out like a book being clapped shut in the cavernous dressing room.

Quinny felt the dam of his tension break. Without thinking he lurched forward and threw a right cross, his gloved hand slamming into Bartley's jaw, causing his father to stumble backward.

Bartley clutched his chin but smiled at Quinny. "It's fight or flight, boyo, and you chose fight. Good man. Now, get out there!"

Although still queasy, Quinny suddenly found himself able to rise and Bartley, joined outside the door by Father Devlin and the official from the athletic commission, pushed the young fighter down the hallway and through the curtain.

Half the crowd, which was ten or fifteen thousand strong, erupted in cheers when Quinny appeared. The other half was there for Tyrus, waving green, black, and yellow flags, but Quinny's contingent overpowered them, chanting "Jim-ee! Jim-ee!" and waving the stars and stripes. Quinny thought that all of Southern Brooklyn must be out there, pulling for him.

He was still sure he was fucked, but he found himself swept up in the moment, and he stopped caring. He smiled idiotically at the crowd. He told himself that being here, having a shot at the Golden Gloves, was pure luck, and he better enjoy it while it lasted. Nobody gave a shit about the boxing since Tyson got locked up, and the amateur scene wasn't drawing real talent, so

Quinny was just the best of a bad crop—and, he knew, riding a wave of suppressed racial animosity. He knew his record was padded out by conquering a bunch of overmatched fat kids who were forced into boxing by overbearing fathers—either to toughen them up or make them lose weight. He'd been the focus of several slobbering articles in the sports sections, his picture featured next to headlines like "He's White and He Can Fight." Local bars organized bus trips to high school gymnasiums to support him in the preliminary matches. He was actually a star, a celebrity. It was crazy.

But now the moment of truth was here . . .

Somehow, Quinny finally stepped between the ropes and entered the ring. From his elevated vantage point, he scanned the sea of faces in the crowd and smiled and raised a glove when he saw Justine, Carlos, Vinny Dago, Lucien Pollution, Joe Damage, Brian 40, Vic Vegas, Franco, and half of the New York hardcore scene packed into a section. His heart soared until he saw that the seat in the front row reserved for his mother was empty.

Nonetheless, the anxiety began to wear off. And then returned when he looked across the ring. Tyrus Raymond was glaring at him, throwing loose punches and dancing from one foot to the other. The tall, lanky Jamaican had a fresh flat-top fade. His onyx skin made a sharp contrast with his yellow tank top and glistened under the ring lights. His eyes showed no sign of fear.

Quinny tried make his own eyes steely, tried to forget that anyone who knew boxing would be sure that he was about to die a death of a thousand jabs. The most fucked part was, Bartley knew this better than anyone. Bartley had spent a decade training Tyrus, just so the cocksucker could backstab the old man, and Quinny, as they got to the top of the mountain. Quinny tried to shake off the attack of despair. Yes, Raymond's reach was longer, his punches were straighter, and his movements were more fluid, but Quinny was far more powerful. Quinny had been hauling scrap metal since he could walk. Quinny hit much, much harder. But, goddammit, you can't hurt what you can't hit, can you?

Fuck it. He would do his job. *No matter what. Never Quit.* He knew the ref wouldn't dare stop it. Everyone had to go home happy. The white working class had learned not to expect winners. They were happy enough with valiant losers. No tall poppies need apply. All Quinny had to do was survive.

When the bald-headed ref went over the rules, Tyrus locked eyes with Quinny and blew him a kiss. Quinny blinked, not expecting such a cheap psych-out attempt from his former brother-in-arms. Before he realized what he was doing, his eyes darted down to the *Daily News* logo printed on the canvas. *What* was *that supposed to be? A camera? A TV? A square with a dot in the center? Fuck!* He realized he'd just given up the psychological advantage in a way that only the greenest rookies did, but when he raised his eyes, Tyrus was looking at the ref.

Quinny wandered back to his corner, a dark feeling consuming him. Bartley saw the defeat in his eyes and reached over the rope and slapped him again, lightly this time. “Son!” his father said. “Choose fight.”

The bell rang.

Quinny plodded out to the center of the ring. Tyrus circled to the left and boxed from distance, peppering his face with jabs, and sidestepping his telegraphed counter hooks. Quinny’s punches came in slow motion. His mind worked in slow motion, unable to make sense of the scene through tunnel vision and vertigo. Though Quinny spent fourteen of his eighteen years on Earth boxing, it looked like this was his first time in the ring. He couldn’t lay a glove on Tyrus, who was piling up the points with jabs to Quinny’s face. *Jesus, I’m embarrassing himself in front of Justine, the Stompers, the whole fucking world.*

The second round began with more of the same. Tyrus came out slick and mixed in right hands with his jabs. Quinny woke up a little once he tasted blood in his mouth. He rushed forward with his guard up and used his strength to push Tyrus into the ropes, pounding the body with short, hard hooks.

In amateur boxing, judges don’t usually score body punches. They like a clean scoring punch that lands to the head with the white stripe along the middle of the glove. Aware of the peculiarities of judging, Tyrus let Quinny bang away at his ribs. The punches hurt, but Tyrus smiled through them. Probably thinking Quinny was a complete idiot for wasting his time with body shots.

Quinny found his groove and kept up the pace, but Tyrus held until the ref called for a break and pulled them apart. When he heard the call "fight," Jimmy Quinn put everything he had behind a left hook to the jaw.

Tyrus saw it coming before Quinny finished thinking about throwing it. The Jamaican ducked under the punch and countered with a right-cross-left-hook combo that knocked Quinny to the floor on his elbow and hip like Burt Reynolds posing for *Playgirl.*

Holy fucking shit! His world was disintegrating around him. He'd never been knocked down in a fight before. He wondered if he ought to stay down. Another three and a half minutes of this would destroy him, but the ref counted so slowly Quinny would have had time for an hour-long nap before the guy got to ten.

Quinny had to finish on his feet. That was the unwritten rule. Nobody wanted a riot on their hands.

Two rounds for Tyrus Raymond. A big zilch for Jimmy Quinn. Quinny needed a knockout to win or at least a knockdown to save face. He would have been less embarrassed if he had shit himself.

Back in his corner, Bartley was near ecstasy. With one minute until the bell rang for

the third and final round, he saw Quinny pulling off the perfect con. "You're putting on an Oscar-worthy performance as a punching bag," he said, shaking his head. "You sneaky son of a bitch."
Quinny's stomach dropped. His dad believed he was playing possum, giving Tyrus a false sense of security and waiting for an opportunity to land a surprise knockout punch. A clever plan. But Quinny was actually trying to win. He had given it his best for six grueling minutes. This was all he had to offer.

Tyrus Raymond was sitting quietly in his corner, as though in meditation. Quinny could feel the confidence emanating from the kid. He didn't need to mop up his sweat or catch his breath. His cornermen didn't even bother to offer advice.

Bartley Quinn stared into his son's eyes. He bit his lip to hide his madman's smile. "Listen for my voice, son," he said. "When I tell you to drop the Bullhammer, you know what to do." He wound up and slapped Quinny in the face again. "Don't fuck this up, boyo!"

The fucking Bullhammer. He can't be serious. Quinny had always thought that punch was nothing more than a Traveller tall tale from a master bullshitter. When he was a kid, Bartley had built up a legend around the punch, described the Bullhammer as a nuclear option left over from the days of bareknuckle boxing, a forgotten technique only used by Gypsy and Traveller knuckle-men in the modern era. It was the punch, Bartley claimed, that flatlined the Guv.

"Imagine your fist is a metal ball attached to the chain that is your arm," a wild-eyed Bartley had told twelve-year-old Quinny. "Take a big step forward with the left foot to generate momentum, then snap your hips to whip the arm like a ball and chain toward your opponent's chin. They'll see what looks like a wide haymaker coming and put up the earmuff defense to protect the sides of his head. It looks like a looping overhand, but, at the last second you turn your fist vertically. If done correctly, the downward rotation of the fist means it lands in the same place a straight cross would. The gloved area over your top two knuckles connects with the point of their chin and knocks them senseless!"

Quinny had tried the punch in sparring a couple of times when he was coming up, but it never worked the way Bartley said it would, and as time went on, he just stuck to the basics and relied on his power.

"The Bullhammer is bull*shit*, isn't it?" Quinny now asked his dad around the mouthpiece.

"Fuck no, it isn't!" Bartley said. "The technique will come to you like fuckin' magic. It's in here." The old man tapped two fingers against Quinny's headgear. "I didn't know I had it until I laid out the Guv'nor. Just wait for my signal and then unleash it!"

From the stool in his corner, Quinny looked out at his crowd. They were white wetbacks, zips, tough Jews, Guidos, construction Pollacks, and plastic Paddies . . . the last of the New York urban white working class. They were living vicariously through him, a promising teenage dirtbag with his whole life ahead of him. If Quinny could win this fight, then they might be able to forget their shitty under-the-table jobs and expired visas and failed plans and pull out an unlikely victory of their own. They needed to believe. Jimmy Quinn was the hope of the outer-borough trash, and he embraced it. *The fucking Bullhammer. This round is going to be different.*

The bell rang and Quinny stood up, marched in, and ate jabs again for the first thirty seconds. He felt like he was reliving the first two rounds. He sensed that the ref might step in and stop the fight as a mercy to him, so he flicked a few jabs of his own to show some life and buy some time.

Tyrus laughed off his lazy jabs. His footwork became livelier, cockier. Quinny felt lightheaded and queasy again, then his dad yelled for the Bullhammer. He chose to fight.

Tyrus moved laterally. Quinny's balance was compromised so he moved with his lead foot forward like a baseball pitcher. He accidentally stepped on the toes of Tyrus's back boot—a completely illegal move—but the ref looked the other way. Tyrus was trapped, pinned like a butterfly.

Quinny swung his arm like David's slingshot and clipped Goliath right on the chin. An electric jolt ran up his hand, to his elbow. He watched, amazed, as Tyrus Raymond's eyes emptied, and the kid bounced off the ropes, then toppled forward onto his face.

Quinny looked around, not sure if the thing actually happened, experiencing reality in slow motion, waiting for someone to wake him up, or for the ref to come over and tell him he was disqualified. The ref, instead, ordered him to a neutral corner, and counted Tyrus Raymond out.

The Garden went mad. Quinny grinned as the ring filled with people around him. Bartley Quinn ran over and shook his boy by the shoulders—the closest they'd ever come to a hug—and screamed, "No more scrapping. You're going pro. We'll make millions."

Tyrus Raymond stayed down. The ringside doctor, Father Devlin, and officials crouched over him.

Greaser Jack joined the in-ring celebration. He probably made a fortune because everybody with a lick of sense bet against the white kid. Quinny raised his hands in victory as beer cups and soda cans began to fly into the ring—Tyrus Raymond's supporters weren't as pleased about his triumph.

The crowd was so loud he almost missed the announcement: *"The winner and 1994 New York Daily News Golden Gloves Heavyweight Champion—Jimmeeeeeeee Quinnnnnnn."*

His picture was on the back page of the sports section the next day.

CHAPTER SIX: NAZI PUNKS FUCK OFF

For the next two weeks, Quinny and Justine Obscene were inseparable, save for the hours he spent scrapping, doing his boxing drills, and sweating his balls off through conditioning exercises at the no-frills gym his dad set up at Quinn and Son Scrap Metal.

The drudgery of rope-skipping wasn't so bad when he escaped into daydreams of Justine, sitting on his front stoop in tiny athletic shorts, drinking a bottle of Manhattan Special (ever since he'd introduced her to the locally made espresso soda, she drank it as often as she could). Swinging a sledgehammer until his upper body felt like Jell-O was tolerable when he knew he'd get to spend time with Justine afterward. They spent every evening together. Justine sat on his lap and they shotgunned weed, drank forty-ounce bottles of Crazy Horse, and listened to demo tapes from bands like 25 ta Life and Darkside NYC.

Justine loved to get high and tell wild stories about her past. To hear her explain it, she was almost literally raised by wolves. She said she was born just outside Soviet Odessa to a pair of abusive alcoholics, who loved the bottle more than little Anya (her birth name) and older brother Vadim. To escape their father's unpredictable rages, the children slept behind the dilapidated house in an unheated shed with the animals.

They fought for whatever the animals ate and lived on that. After several years of this, the authorities caught on and sent her parents up the river. Anya and Vadim were media sensations, on the front page of Russian-language newspapers and TV shows the world over. As celebrity charity cases among post-communist exiles, they were saved when the Malenkos of Montreal adopted them from a dingy Russian orphans' home. When she turned fourteen, she hopped on a bus to San Francisco to become Justine Obscene.

She explained why by name-checking the Marquis de Sade, and Quinny pretended he knew what the hell she was talking about. There was a local metal band called DeSade, so it must've been badass. Was he being a poser for pussy? Yeah, but Quinny didn't care. He was poised to turn pro, and with this give-no-fucks crust punk goddess as his girl, the life he had always dreamed of was actually within his grasp.

After this particular version of her origin story—eventually, he'd notice the details changed frequently—Quinny held her as she cried until they both succumbed to drunken sleep on the mattress in his bedroom.

He knew, of course, that Justine was lying. For starters, she was Black, and the strange accent she sometimes had definitely did not sound Russian. No lingering feral wolf stuff either. She walked, ate, talked, acted like a person who was used to people and civilization. And the day they met, before they went on the mission for Tommy's shoes, she told him she was seventh-generation Afro-Canadian from the oldest Free Black settlement in Nova Scotia. She had also, in her letters before he met her, contradicted that story. Most of the West Coast punk kids believed that she was the daughter of General Field Marshal Cinque and Patricia Hearst because that's how she passed herself off.

Whatever the truth was, her imagination and the way she told a story excited him. It was clever. Resourceful. Maybe not trustworthy, but that would change once she understood they were two halves of a whole.

Quinny never cared about a girl like this before. Longing and tenderness were new emotions for him. He wanted to be with Justine all the time. He'd follow her anywhere. He knew in his gut that she felt something for him. He knew he was her safe space, and he felt like a hero of some kind when he enveloped her thin limbs, as delicate as bird bones, in his muscled arms.

Since the Golden Gloves triumph, Justine was stressing about capturing a climactic scene for her documentary. The key was that the Stompers needed to look like they were good guys under their frightening exteriors. She decided that the best way to show that was following them as they hunted down racist, fascist elements in the scene and beat down Nazi punks.

Quinny was eager to give her exactly what she wanted. He was already lost in a fantasy of him and Justine as king and queen of the underground. He saw how his whole life was going to go. The stuff of legends. She'd tour with her documentary at every college campus and punk squat in the country, and he'd drive the van. With a pro boxing license, they could pick a town somewhere and he'd fight their local ticket-selling hero. He'd knock that chump's ass out and get booed out of the arena while Justine filmed the whole thing. The seedy underbelly of low-stakes local boxing—just the right subject matter. It would be his gift to her. Maybe he'd learn how to shoot video and help.

Every now and then, when she would seem annoyed at his affections or would disappear for several hours and not tell him where she'd gone, Quinny was gripped by an unaccountable dread. Like, maybe she was just using him. Maybe as soon as her movie was done, she would start making excuses and leave him. But he couldn't believe it. He thought of how she cried in his arms, and he knew this was the real thing. He longed to tell Justine that he loved her, but he sensed that the time wasn't quite right. First, he had to break a Nazi face in her honor. Give her the perfect ending.

When he heard that Carnivore was playing a reunion show at L'Amour, he knew this was it. Boston's Bricklayer, Dare to Defy from Philly, and Brooklyn bands Indecision, Dishonor, Out of Line, Purge NYC, Shutdown, Step Aside, and

Subjection were opening. There was a one hundred percent chance of chaos with that lineup.

He told Justine to get her camera ready and prepare for a bloodbath.

They rode on the B9 bus from Avenue L and Nostrand. They sipped Cisco bum wine in a brown paper bag from a straw. He blasted the new Indecision demo tape from a boom box while Justine conducted a video interview. The camera made him self-conscious, and he flubbed his answers. With the lens pointed at his face, it occurred to him that he wasn't particularly interesting.

She was raised by dogs. He was raised by a scrap metaller and a cashier who was always asleep on the couch. He was a Graveyard Stomper because . . . he had no fucking idea why. It just seemed cool. It came with a jacket from a real gangster. He was good at fighting. He liked going to hardcore shows. He didn't like getting jumped. As a kid, he took beatings from Black kids pissed off over the racial murders in Howard Beach and Bensonhurst. He also took beatings from white kids because he was a weirdo who listened to "kill your mother, kill your father, worship Satan" music. He took beatings from Bartley indirectly when he overmatched him in the ring against guys way tougher than him. He went home and took his father's beatings directly, too. Quinny was tired of being the nail. He wanted to be the hammer.

He felt like more of a jerkoff after every dopey answer he gave.

He got drunker and drunker, and mumbled stiff I-dunnos until Justine took pity on him and put the camera away. She kissed his head and thanked him like a disappointed grandmother.

They got off at Fourteenth Avenue and Sixtieth Street—a part of Brooklyn he called Garbagetown, USA—and walked three blocks to L'Amour through a warehouse district in awkward silence.

The Graveyard Stompers were representing in front of the club. Skinhead Carlos was shirtless, wearing red braces to match the red laces on his Docs. He holstered the Hammer of Justice through one of the belt loops of his jeans and didn't care who saw it. Joe Damage dressed for battle (or his on-camera debut) in French-cuffed Levi's, a small Champion T-shirt that fit like a half shirt, and a steel chain fastened around his waist with a bicycle lock. He wore a pair of construction gloves like the old-timers from the Wolfpack and United Blood.

Cyrus, who wore the same thing every day, was selling bags of something. He was in his customary pristine white Hanes T-shirt—oversized, of course—and navy-blue Dickies work pants. Nobody knew what Cyrus had against laundry, but the guy never washed a shirt. Instead, he bought a fresh one each day, took it out of the package, and changed into it on the sidewalk outside the Modell's in King's Plaza. The perks of drug dealing. A fighting pit bull named Bamm-Bamm was always by his side. Cyrus rescued/liberated/stole the animal a few months back from some deadbeat who owed him money. Bamm-Bamm was a scary dog, but Quinny saw him get fucked up by a regular-ass housecat one night at some dude's apartment. When Cyrus came by to drop off some coke, Bamm-Bamm barged through the partially opened front door and locked his jaw around the customer's cat. It took two of the hardest dudes he ever met—Cyrus and Franco—to get Bamm-Bamm to release the cat. Turns out they were rescuing Bamm-Bamm. That cat had scratched the fuck out of him. Score that round 10-8 for the cat. Quinny never sweated the monster pit bull after that.

If you could believe it, Tommy looked the coolest of all in a Confusion "Storm the Walls of Sanity" T-shirt and Greaser Jack's original Graveyard Stompers club jacket from the '50s. Quinny gave the jacket to Tommy when they made the kid a brother. Everybody in the crew, including Quinny, wanted it, but Tommy was the only one small enough to fit into it. People were fucking tiny back in the '50s. None of the neighborhood guys ever tried to take it off Tommy because everyone knew who gave it to him.

Tommy couldn't fight for shit, but he was a clever son of a bitch who earned his place in spades.

By the summer of '94, Carlos and Quinny had recruited a sizeable crew, but it didn't amount to much except manpower. The

Graveyard Stompers needed cash for records, show tickets, weapons, boots and braces, shit, even sandwiches—not all these kids had cabinets stocked with healthy snacks. Half of them barely had parents.

One day, Tommy asked, "Who sells drugs to the freaks?"

Carlos and Quinny looked at each other.

"Not like . . . actual freaks. Punks, skins, metalheads, ravers, club kids, skaters, goths, dirtbags. Outcasts. Where do they buy their shit?" he wondered out loud.

The little fuck was right. No way were those kids with candy-colored hair and eyebrow rings driving out to Bensonhurst to score from the Cropsey Avenue Boys, Dario Fortunato's mafiosos-in-training. And they'd be risking their lives trying to cop in Flatbush from the Decepticons outside the Vanderveer Projects.

"So why not us?" Tommy asked.

Shit. Why NOT us?

Tommy's friend Jelani from the chess team was Decepticon affiliated—he agreed to be their connect. He handed gym bags full of weed to Quinny from a drop locker at Our Lady of Annihilation Boxing Club and Carlos picked up the hard drugs and club drugs from a mob-owned auto body shop in Coney Island. The split was the same: the gangsters fronted the supply, and the Stompers got one free bag for every three they sold. *Three for them. One for us. Everybody's happy, everybody's paid* . . . as long as they coughed up the cash and didn't cause any problems.

Quinny and Carlos passed the drugs off to fellow Stompers who got a free bag to sell for themselves for every three *they* sold for the GYS. The underground finally had a safe and reliable drug connection, and the Graveyard Stompers graduated to a real gang.

Justine practically squealed with delight at the goonish scene. Her interviews were far more compelling when the camera was pointed at something besides Quinny, who seemed to start sweating and stammering any time the film rolled. A forty-ounce of St. Ides was, not surprisingly, the key to getting Brian 40, their most prolific tagger, talking, but malt liquor also worked on Chris Newfie and Francesco, who wore some goofy-ass sandals he brought back from Italy. Vic Vegas wore a suit and didn't need anything to get him talking. He was down with GYS, but he was only peripherally involved in the hardcore scene. He hung around to pick up girls outside the shows and take them to the Marine Park Inn. Soon they unleashed their pro-wrestling-worthy trash talk and cut promos for the camera. Phil Core ran up to the camera and screamed, "Graveyard Stompers, Ninety-Four! Who's calling the shots now, motherfucker?" Justine was psyched—she told Quinny she could already put together a trailer with the footage she had.

The boys looked the part. It was only a matter of time before they did the business. To ease them along, Justine handed out blunts with what she said was a crack rock stuffed into the end "like a diamond in a ring setting." They hit the blunts hard and kept clowning for the camera.

That was about when everybody's memory got hazy. Their stories never matched up after the blunt. Maybe they just didn't want to remember.

Later, the prosecution—and the newspapers—claimed some dumbfuck white boy from Jersey wearing a confederate flag Pantera T-shirt walked up to a group of skinheads, Sieg Heiled, and screamed, "I hate Jews too." It might have been "niggers" or "spics"—nobody really knew—if you asked ten people who were there, you'd hear ten different versions.

Anyway, having just said some racist shit to a bunch of guys in skinhead gear, this dumbfuck probably soon noticed that there were a lot of Black and Brown faces attached to those boots and braces and realized he fucked up.

Quinny was there, but this story never seemed familiar to him in the retelling. He only knew the rest from Justine's video.

Carlos set it off by returning the Hitler salute with a hammer in his hand before bringing it down on Dumbfuck's shoulder. The poor fool fell onto the asphalt and Joe Damage did his best Pelé impression with the soccer kicks. Bamm-Bamm bit Dumbfuck's head because he crawled too close to Cyrus. Dumbfuck returned to his feet and stood dazed, swaying, elbows protecting his ears, not knowing what would come next.

Quinny knew this was his moment. He felt the camera on him as he closed in on the guy. His stiff jab opened Dumbfuck's guard, then he bingo'd him with the hardest Bullhammer he ever landed. It was like he meant for the punch to go straight through the dude's face. He put all of his 212 pounds behind that punch.

Dumbfuck got slept.

Dumbfuck fell backwards.

Dumbfuck cracked his skull and bled like a broken water main.

Dumbfuck stopped moving.

A bouncer called the police, and the boys ran in every direction. Quinny stayed at the venue with Justine, who quietly stroked his hair.

"The guy was an anti-Semite and said racist shit," she said. "Don't worry, I got it on tape."

"Good," Quinny said. "Fuck that Nazi. I hope he's dead."

The next day one newspaper's headline was, "F**k That Nazi, I Hope He's Dead." Another had a doofy-looking picture of Quinny posing for a Golden Gloves promo in boxing trunks, hands wrapped, with the headline, "I Hope He's Dead."

The video was all over the television. It was a beautiful punch under any circumstances. Miraculous, considering he was blackout drunk at the time.

CHAPTER SEVEN: INJUSTICE SYSTEM

There was no way in hell a jury would convict a teenage kid for punching a racist piece of shit doing Nazi salutes in the street, right? Brooklyn would never turn their back on Quinny for a white supremacist. This was one of the most ethnically and racially diverse places on Earth—that shit doesn't fly in the borough of Kings. So, against the wishes of his lawyer, Quinny refused to take the prosecution's deal for a cup-of-coffee sentence. He rolled the dice and went to trial. *Fuck Nazis, and fuck going to jail for even a minute.* He was going to live the hobo life with Justine.

Quinny had reason to be confident. Father Devlin testified on his behalf as a character witness—that was worth a million dollars. The local priest was practically a saint. He ran a soup kitchen that fed fifteen hundred people a day, his church was a sanctuary for undocumented immigrants, and his scrappy gym turned street kids into world-class boxers. He had friends in high places, too. With the priest on board, Quinny could add Reverend Sharpton and Cardinal O'Connor as potential character witnesses. Even Greaser Jack Fortunato did his part, sending associates to "reach out" to jurors and make sure they did the right thing by Quinny. Everyone rallied around Quinny because they agreed he was a generally goodhearted kid who sometimes got in above his head.

Never was that clearer than when Quinny took the stand. When the prosecutor asked if he thought he'd get into a street fight that night, Quinny naively said yes. When asked if he was the one who threw the punch that killed the guy doing the Hitler salute, Quinny said yes. When asked if he knew the brawl was being filmed, Quinny said yes. The prosecutor paused dramatically and asked Quinny if, once upon a time, he threw hunks of watermelon at Black protestors marching down Eighteenth Avenue. Quinny didn't say anything.

He looked around the courtroom for an assist, but no one would meet his gaze. The jury box, he now realized, were not *exactly* his peers. He counted seven Black jurors, a couple of Asian ones, and two white ones. Quinny's stomach sank, and his face started burning. No words would come to him. He suddenly felt lightheaded.

The prosecutor asked again. "Did you and your friends go to Bensonhurst and throw watermelon at peaceful marchers during a candlelight vigil for murdered Black teenager Yusef Hawkins?"

Quinny visibly squirmed on the stand and the prosecutor got permission to treat him as a hostile witness. Quinny pounded the wood on the witness stand with his fist in a suitably hostile manner.

"I was only twelve!" Quinny shouted. "What the hell do you know about it? You didn't grow up where I did. That racial shit was fucked up. Not for you, though. You had a nice life. You were safe in your nice private school. You know how many times me and my friends got jumped because of what happened to Yusef Hawkins? Back then, we were guilty of being white, no questions asked. Even the Latin and Asian kids caught beatings with us for being white—all because some pieces of shit from Bensonhurst got jealous and killed a Black kid who was fucking one of their girls. What did that have to do with us? We were tired of getting our asses kicked. Tired of losing."

"Is that a yes, or no?" the prosecutor asked.

"It's fuck you," Quinny replied.

A groan rang out across the courtroom, after which Bartley was quickly escorted out. Out of the corner of his eye, Quinny saw Father Devlin drop his head into his hands.

Okay, change of plan.

Suddenly, Quinny answered yes to every shitty thing he'd ever done. He realized the truth, the whole truth, and nothing but the truth was the way to go. The jury would share his moral compass. Everybody hated Nazis, he reasoned, and New Yorkers hated Nazis even more, since they're all just a generation or two away from being outsiders. Quinny knew they'd cut him a break. If he was on the jury, he wouldn't convict a guy like him for doing what he did. The only time he answered no was when asked if he knew the victim was the son of a township cop in

Bumfuck, New Jersey. He got crushed on the stand.

It couldn't have gone worse. They made it sound like he was looking to kill this guy, like it was all premeditated. Reverend Al and the Cardinal never showed.

The gavel came down hard and fast.

Twenty years.

Not an ounce of sympathy from the judge.

***

Ridgehaven State Correctional Facility wasn't at all like Quinny thought it would be. He was scared shitless at the idea of having to fight his way through the entire inmate population. On the bus ride there, he tried to remember Greaser Jack's advice about who to sit next to in the cafeteria, who to bribe, who to avoid. But when he walked through the front gates, he was greeted like a goddamn celebrity. His fellow inmates whooped it up for him on the block, banging their metal cups against the bars. They even gave him a nickname—the Nazi Killer.

There was no Aryan presence in New York State Prison, so there was no downside to the nickname either. Quinny thought he could do his time, as the cons said, standing on his head.

He killed a cop's kid. That's bigtime outlaw shit on the inside, so he was a hero to the other cons. Quinny didn't need to worry that the screws would be out to get him either. The corrections officers didn't side with their law enforcement brothers—half of them hated the police department. (They still held a grudge from when they washed out applying for the job themselves. How else would someone wind up a CO?) They were cool as fuck to him and treated him fairly. No better or no worse than the next guy.

Quinny kept his head down but had an easygoing "what's up" and a nod ready for anybody who had one for him. He joined the prison boxing program and found a home. Nobody fucked with him. He had no beefs.

He settled into his routine and the months went by, faster and faster, one year, two years passed like nothing. He got a card from Bartley on his twentieth birthday. If he could make it through seven years as a model inmate, he could get out then—and with good time, he might get early parole and could be out even sooner.

But in year six he met Peralta, and it all went ass over elbows. Peralta looked like a real-life superhero standing six foot six, and nearly three hundred pounds of pure ripped muscle. He had the face of a movie star—picture a super jacked Antonio Banderas with a neatly slicked back ponytail, on a mission to be the alpha male of the prison.

Whenever Quinny bench pressed in the yard, that 'roided-out Dominican hulk Peralta was there to add an extra plate to each side of his bar and show him up. When Quinny deadlifted four plates for reps, Peralta was right behind him, ready to add another forty-five pounds to each side. When Quinny did chin-ups, there was

Peralta doing chin-ups with his legs wrapped around some inmate for added weight.

Quinny paid him no mind. He was gonna be out after the first parole hearing, at twenty-five years old—still in his fighting prime. He'd track down Justine and finish where they left off.
Then Peralta joined the boxing club.

Inmates love porno mags, WWF wrestling on TV, and when a cop gets shot in a movie. A live boxing match between fellow inmates might be the one thing they enjoy more.

Prison boxers are tough, but most of them came to the game too late in life. They don't have the savvy of a boxer who has spent thousands of hours in the ring honing his craft. Prison boxers don't have proper head movement, they have difficulty learning to roll with the punches, and they don't know how to handle the tension and get fatigued from adrenaline dumps. A seasoned boxer like Quinny could maintain emotional balance. He treated punching someone in the face and getting punched in the face like a job. It *was* his job, day in, day out. Jailhouse sluggers drop their hands to admire their work after landing a good punch. *Terrible habits.*

Now Quinny was slated to fight Peralta for the prison heavyweight title. The new guy was a 20-1 underdog. Quinny was used to defending the jailhouse title against other cons. He took it easy in the ring with these guys. He played a little defense, let them tire themselves out, and landed just enough to win and let the other guy keep his dignity. He always raised the other guy's hands at the end as a sign of good will. He made everybody feel good. That was Jimmy Quinn's thing.

A beast of a man who outweighed Quinny by at least fifty pounds, Peralta looked so intimidating no one ever fucked with him. A guy that size never needs to throw hands, so he's likely to grossly overestimate his ability as a fighter. But as Quinny watched Peralta spar one day, he discovered it was worse than he thought. Peralta couldn't fight at all. His punches were garbage. He gassed out early. His engorged muscles stiffened his movements. Quinny determined that he'd been hit harder by children.

One Dominican boss from Inwood dropped so much coin on Peralta that the betting odds changed to dead even. Gambling in prison gets you killed faster than anything else, even gang affiliation. Quinny wanted no part of it. He came to terms with his role quickly, losing this thing for the sake of peace. It was just a jailhouse title, not worth the aggravation. He'd be out soon enough. Just let Peralta hold the trinket. He was ready to take this dive.

Then, out of nowhere, the odds swung back to 10-1 in Quinny's favor. Greaser Jack wanted a fair fight, and he was willing to pay for it. The New York underworld played out in microcosm: the Dominicans ran shit, and the Italians had a hard time accepting the fact.

Bartley had been almost right about the mafia. Five years on, the old syndicates were practically dead. Who wanted to be a mobster in the twenty-first century? Young Italian American men had much better options. Fucking garbage men were getting paid a hundred grand a year. Who was going to risk getting his head blown off or a prison bid for the same money a garbageman makes? Quinny knew the mafia was done, the other inmates knew the mafia was done, but Greaser Jack didn't know it—or at least he pretended not to. His bet put Quinny in a situation, and the last thing Quinny needed before his parole hearing was a situation.

On fight day, the inmates were going wild outside the ring. They knew this wasn't just another exhibition. Peralta vs. Quinn had bigger consequences. Peralta marched confidently to the ring and flexed his muscles. Quinny had no banter for the onlookers. He looked like he just woke up from a long nap.

The bell rang and Quinny let Peralta get some inside shots off, then lightly tapped him back to the body. The big guy backed up like a dump truck. Quinny circled and let him miss a few swings. Peralta rushed in and grabbed Quinn, pushing him against the ropes. Quinn was shocked by his strength. He felt like he was wrestling a cement pillar. Peralta, too close to land effectively, smothered his own punches. Quinny circled out of the clinch and intentionally missed with ones and twos. Peralta pumped out power shots—hooks and uppercuts thrown with maximum effort and zero setup. Quinny threw a right hand and stood flat-footed in front of his opponent, which allowed Peralta to hook off. Quinny felt those. He was visibly rocked, and the inmates went crazy. Peralta had some serious pop, but he didn't know how to follow it up for a finish. Quinny broke off a left hook to the ribs and one to the face to make it look like he was trying. After three minutes of action, the bell rang as Peralta bull-rushed him into the ropes.

With one eye swollen shut, Peralta walked to the wrong corner between rounds, which infuriated him. He turned a deep shade of purple. Quinny tried to make eye contact with the ref as the Dominican monster heaved into a plastic bucket in his corner. All those muscles needed oxygen, and Peralta was physically unprepared. Quinny knew he'd have to do a flop as soon as the bell rang for the second round, or he'd be dealing with real consequences from the Uptown bosses instead of empty threats from the mafia.

Unfortunately, the ref looked like he wasn't going to allow the steroid freak to continue and come out for round two. His corner waved the ref off and tried to give Peralta water, but he threw that up too. A cold sweat came over Quinny. He felt like he was about to take a giant shit right there in the ring. *This can't be happening,* he kept telling himself. But as sure as he was convicted for punching a Nazi in Brooklyn, it happened. Peralta pulled a Roberto Duran and quit in the ring.

No mas.

The referee put the title belt on a stunned Quinny. He couldn't even fake a reaction and let the inmates believe he was happy about winning.

Quinny got his guts cut out with Stanley knives that night. The Washington Heights Boys farmed the job out to neighborhood guys Quinny grew up with. He never saw it coming. They stuck him like Julius Caesar and left him in a puddle. The CO who responded delivered the message: he should have taken the fall. Dominicans don't play, and mob connections don't mean shit anymore.

That night Quinny sat up in a prison hospital bed, thinking, accepting what had happened. It was as close as he ever came to meditating. He knew his shot at good time, or a parole hearing, was over. He'd have to serve the full twenty, probably in protective custody. They were all coming for him. He would be lucky now just to survive, and he was only going to survive by fucking motherfuckers up. From here on out he was doing it the hard way.

CHAPTER EIGHT: STREET JUSTICE

The bus from Rikers Island dropped Quinny off, along with a dozen or so newly released inmates, somewhere on Queens Boulevard. *Rego Park? Maybe Kew Gardens? Who knows?* He was happy just to be in the city again. He stepped onto the curb and looked around, walked up the sidewalk a ways, ignoring the other cons. He craned his neck to take in the blue sky and breathe the familiar air. The constant background noise of traffic and human activity felt like home. Many of the cars gliding along the street looked space-aged to him, glossy and bubble-shaped, but otherwise the city was the same.

He just needed to be picked up. Quinny glanced around the boulevard and saw nothing. Bartley had given his word that he'd be here. Even he wouldn't blow something as big as his kid getting out of the joint after two decades. But Quinny's neck started to get hot as he realized that was just what was happening.

Quinny loitered for an hour, getting increasingly pissed, watching as the other cons were collected by friends and loved ones. A couple had limos waiting for them, hired strippers peeking out of the sunroofs with bottles in hand. Others had exuberant family reunions in the street with hand-drawn signs that said, "Welcome

Home" and round, gray-haired mothers who held on much too tight when they hugged.

Quinny stood alone. He tried not to let bitter irony overtake him, but it was a real gut-shot. He was a high-profile case, a jailhouse boxing legend, the subject of an HBO documentary called *Nazi Killer*, and—based on the letters he got from admirers across the country—pretty damned popular.

And yet, when it really mattered, no one gave a fuck.

Luckily, the Department of Corrections provided MetroCards for sad sacks who had to take the subway home. He began walking.

In a parked car's side window, he saw his reflection and, in spite of himself, he paused and stared. Everything that was happening, that had happened, seemed to hit him at once. *The kid who last walked these streets is dead and buried.* A bearded, nearly middle-aged man looked back at him in the afternoon sun. There was considerable gray in his dark beard and his once-subtle widow's peak now formed a sharp point at the front of his skull. His black hair, in need of a trim, was also dusted with gray. Above the beard, his eyes were nestled in the creases of a million pained grimaces and his once-lean cheeks were padded with accumulated scar tissue. His whole body, for that matter, was transformed: coated in jailhouse tattoos and so thickened from prison iron that his chest and shoulders strained the seams of the white, state-issued, extra-large T-shirt.

He looked away and kept going. He felt a giant, empty hole inside him expanding, swallowing his anger, overtaking his loneliness. He realized that the feeling was not philosophical, but chemical: a nicotine craving so fierce that for a moment he forgot about everything else. Stopping right there, tearing a hole in the clear, plastic, personal-property envelope he'd received at discharge, he pulled a twenty-dollar bill from his stash. A yellow bodega sign beckoned in the distance and Quinny made for it, somehow managing to cross the notorious Boulevard of Death without getting run over.

When he got to the place, he was disappointed to learn that, despite the classic bodega sign, it wasn't a bodega at all. Inside it was just a corner store. He felt annoyance spiraling into rage and fought it down. Bodegas were part of New York's identity, something he had just assumed would always be. They were owned and operated by dudes from Puerto Rico or the Dominican Republic and straddled the line between different worlds. They were where you could get Malta soft drinks, *El Diario*, the Spanish daily paper, and a sexual aid called La Piedra, a rock to stick up your cock-hole for raging hard-ons. The good ones had hot Latin-Caribbean food, and the really good ones also had weed, coke, and heroin. Corner stores, like this shit hole, are owned by dudes from Yemen. Muslims who don't sell beer or pork. They deal in coffee, lotto tickets, synthetic weed, and fucking breakfast sandwiches.

When Quinny had seen the bodega sign he had immediately decided what his first meal on the outside would be. He had spent half his life listening to Latin Kings and *Ñetas* talk up the bodega *medianoche* Cubano sandwich. But as the door closed behind him, he looked at the clerk's dead black eyes and knew that that dream, like everything else, had just turned into shit. He approached the counter, glancing around the cramped, smelly market. He cleared his throat and said, "Marlboro reds."

As the clerk stirred to life his eyes swept over the bulk of Quinny's shoulders and chest, and the prison tats darkening the giant arms. The man was trying to decide if this customer could spell trouble. He reached up and retrieved the smokes from an overhead rack, casually showing the underarm stain on his T-shirt, and unleashing a reek of BO as he did so.

"Fifteen fifty," the man said as he slapped the red-and-white package onto the counter.

Quinny locked eyes with the clerk for two full seconds.

"Just the smokes, man," he said.

The clerk looked back at him defiantly. "Yes. Fifteen fifty."

Quinny's head began to buzz. He felt that he was at a crossroads. He could drag this fucking rat over the counter, take the smokes and just walk out—or he could play the game he was supposed to play. He knew that inflation had to have occurred while he was inside, but he also knew that assholes like this would charge a thousand bucks for a pack of smokes if they could.

The guy looked at Quinny nervously, as if he could see the notions warring against each other inside the ex-con's head.

Finally, Quinny remembered the three deep breaths strategy he'd been taught in mandatory anger management class. The shit actually worked. By the time he let out his third long exhale—with the clerk peering at him in confusion—he felt calmness wash over him. He replaced his outrage at the cost of the cigarettes with the thought of all the money he'd saved by not smoking for twenty years on the inside.

He slapped the twenty onto the well-worn counter-top and slid it toward the man. "Keep the change, my friend," he said. "And gimme a pack of matches."

He picked up the smokes and matches and walked out. *A free man for five minutes, and I'm already started throwing around twenties like Diamond Jim Brady.*

He said a quiet *thank you* to Greaser Jack as he exited the store. It was Greaser Jack who had told him to kick smoking, one way or another, to survive inside. It was Greaser Jack who had inspired Quinny to live like a monk while he did his bid, partaking of nothing but food and drink. "You can't let another inmate have leverage over you," Jack had told him, "And addictions are leverage." Quinny had seen this proven true time after time. Predatory cons eventually pulled some mark into a card game—

another thing you should never do—and once the fool flipped a card, he was toast. Cigarettes were currency on the inside. Guys lived and died for smokes. A fool played a little poker for a pack to kill the time and the next thing he knew he owed his ass or something worse—a favor.

So, for two decades, Quinny endured the nicotine cravings and boredom. He did push-ups. He read books. He shadowboxed. He jerked off thinking about the girls he didn't seal the deal with when he was a teenager. He gripped the top bar of his cell door with his fingertips and did pull-ups. But he never touched the prison hooch, the illicit baggies of dope, or the ubiquitous cigarettes.

He made his way back across the Boulevard of Death on the off chance that Bartley was still going to find his way here. Then, standing on the sidewalk, after two decades of self-denial, he let himself relax.

His first cigarette gave him a head rush that made him feel like he was high and about to be knocked out at the same time. He wondered if he was going to faint right here on the sidewalk. But when he was done, he chain-smoked two more. People walking by tried not to make eye contact with the hulking prison thug fiendishly sucking on his Marlboros. Then he began to feel nauseated. Then he dropped the pack of smokes and was holding his stomach. Then he had slumped against a steel signpost and was puking out his guts onto the pavement.

When it finally stopped, and he was able to stand up again, Quinny found that he was in a good mood. The whole thing felt like freedom. He wiped the vomit out of his beard and walked down the sidewalk, away from the splattered remnants of a jailhouse baloney sandwich. As he sauntered along, he heard the tap of a fist on a car horn, and looked up and stopped, saying, under his breath, "Great timing, Pop."

Quinny looked at the Dodge Ram truck he had known his whole life, now coated in twenty years of scratches and general neglect. Bartley had pulled the vehicle to a stop in front of a hydrant. Quinny turned on his heel and reached for the door handle.

"Sorry, son," Bartley said as the door opened. "I was held up. It's good to see you out, boyo."

Quinny tried not to show what he was thinking as he climbed in. Bartley's voice was blown out and without the Dodge Ram—if they'd just passed each other on the street—Quinny wouldn't have recognized his own father. The man's face—he saw as he settled into the stained, rusty front seat and ruined the only pair of pants he owned—had become ancient and wasted. But what gave Quinny a real chill was his father's demeanor. Bartley seemed almost shy. If Quinny's time inside taught him anything, it was what a victim looked like. His dad had become prey.

"You got a place to stay?" Bartley asked, looking ahead, smacking the turn signal down as he moved the pickup into traffic.

Quinny's eyes narrowed. "I thought I'd stay in my old room, for a little while at least, until I can get a stake."

"The thing is," Bartley mumbled, looking too hard at the road, "I had to sell the house when your mother left. Nothing I could do about it. Had to give her half and put my half into the business."

Quinny knew what was coming next.

"I'm staying at work, you see—just temporary. And there's nowhere . . ." Bartley's words trailed off. His obvious humiliation made Quinny feel a little better about being thrown out in the street like garbage. The old man had no choice in the matter.

"I'll find somewhere to crash. It's not a problem," Quinny said. "Carlos is in Jersey. Reardon's in Manhattan. I'm gonna see Justine tonight, but it's been a while. She might not want to play house with a dude fresh out of the joint." Then he had a thought. "Actually, you know what? The owner of Marine Park Inn reached out and offered me a security gig and a free room. Turns out the neighborhood's Ultra-Orthodox Jews want to help the Nazi Killer get back on his feet. At least somebody cares."

Bartley laughed—or something that sounded like stage eight cancer came out of the old man's mouth. "That place is a hot sheets," he said, shaking his head, causing loose skin to flap on his face. "You don't want to stay there. Too dangerous."

Quinny scoffed. *Did this motherfucker forget where his kid spent the last 7,665 nights?* "Look, Pop, I don't want to make a whole thing out of it. I'll just sleep on the floor of the shop until I figure something out."

Bartley looked pained. "There's no shop anymore," he said, his voice barely audible. "They took it for unpaid debts, those fucks. Jack Fortunato's guys. I'm just an employee now. I sleep in the back seat of a thirty-two-year-old truck inside the gate of the junkyard I used to *own.* And I have to look at it every day and make money for the new greaseball owner."

"Wait," Quinny said, feeling sick all over again. "Back up. How the fuck did this happen?"

Bartley braked the truck at a red light. The idling motor made the vehicle rattle in a hundred places. It sounded like it could throw a rod at any moment.

"I don't want any trouble," Bartley said.

Quinny laughed. It was the same old Bartley after all. The old man had an angle. He was trying to bait Quinny into getting involved.

"You see," Bartley said, his eyes now bright as they darted over to make sure his son was paying attention. "I hit sixty grand on a parlay. A couple of games in the FA Cup. Leicester City winning the league, and the Tyson Fury fight with Klitschko. Real Cinderella shit. But the guy who takes the action down at Scruffy Murphy's paid me out twenty grand and told me I was beat on the other forty, and to go fuck myself. Forty grand could change our lives. You know what I mean?"

Quinny knew what he meant. "Who's the guy?"

"Never mind," Bartley said. "You don't know him. You've been away a long time."

"What's his name?"

"LoDuca. Antonio LoDuca."

"Tony Dukes?" Quinny shouted, slapping the cracked vinyl dashboard of the Ram. "You let a beef stew like Tony Dukes take forty grand out of your pocket? What the fuck happened to you?"

"Life happened," Bartley said, making the truck lurch forward. "I'm not a young bull like you anymore. When they hand me a shit sandwich, I gotta eat it."

Quinny grunted at the flattery. He knew that Bartley was manipulating him, maneuvering him into getting involved in a conflict that would probably turn into a nightmare. But, as he thought about it, he couldn't imagine not getting involved.

CHAPTER NINE: WORLDS APART

Quinny didn't see a bell for Justine's apartment, but when he approached the building, the door opened automatically. In the center of the black marble lobby, a young, uniformed doorman sat surrounded by screens at what looked like a military command station.

"Can I help you?" he said.

"Uh," Quinny stammered, "I'm Jimmy Quinn. I'm here to see Justine Obscene. She's in apartment nineteen." His face reddened and he felt ridiculous after rattling off what sounded like a Dr. Seuss rhyme.

The doorman smiled. "One moment, please. Let me notify her that you're here."

The doorman called Justine from a landline telephone. Quinny heard her say, "Send him up!" from the other end of the phone.

He entered the elevator. He went to punch in the floor number and discovered there were no buttons in this elevator. The doorman's voice came over an intercom saying, "It's not *manual*," in an incredulous manner. "Hold up, sir, and I'll enter your destination."

Quinny watched the doors whisper shut and felt the elevator rising. When the doors opened, he realized he was stepping directly *into* Justine's apartment. The whole floor was her apartment. *Definitely room for me to sleep.*

“Quinny! In here!” Justine shouted from the living room.

He felt the pain of his arthritic fingers trembling.

The windows stretched from floor to ceiling in her gigantic loft. The floors were covered with an elegant ebony hardwood. Her furniture was futuristic looking. The walls were decorated with posters of her movies, but somehow, it didn’t look braggy. *This place must have cost a fortune.* He found her sitting on a giant white leather couch across from an enormous *Nazi Killer* promo poster. It was a blown-up image of his mug shot photo when he was eighteen: shaved head, massive sideburns, and an indignant smirk. He was transfixed by the image of himself for a few moments, then tore his gaze away and looked at Justine.

It was like the situation with his dad all over again. If he didn’t know this was Justine, he never would have guessed it was her. He knew, vaguely, that she was close to fifty years old now, but she seemed to have stopped time—apparently by inhabiting another body. She looked like she was trying on another woman’s face with a symmetrical, upturned nose, pillowy lips, and a lifted brow that made her look perpetually startled. Her hair was maroon and in short twists. She sat with her legs crossed and wore black sweatpants with a bandana-print halter top, which was stretched taut over tits that were two or three times the size of the ones Quinny remembered. She was speed-texting on her phone and didn't even look up as he entered the room.

Quinny felt self-conscious wearing his dad's brown suit, like a child playing dress-up to impress a girl who didn't even bother to change out of sweats.

He took a heavy breath and cleared his throat.

Justine's expression changed slightly. Still not looking up, she said, "Grab a beer from the fridge. Make yourself comfy. I just need a sec." She continued typing and said, "I'm talking to this Viking biker guy . . . real racist piece of shit . . . militia . . . makes meth . . . loves *Nazi Killer.* He's gonna be a great subject."

"Sounds cool," Quinny said, settling on the end of the sofa. "I gotta catch up on some of your movies."

"Yeah," she said, still buried in her phone. "I'll get you a copy of *Save the Unfortunates . . .*" Both thumbs were flying again, and she was biting her bottom lip.

"Cool," he said. "Look, I see this is a bad time and you're busy. I got a thing, anyway. That's why I'm wearing the suit."

She heard the anger creeping into his voice, apparently, and sent her text and looked up at him. Her eyes were the same at least. He could see the age lines around them. She said, "I'm so rude! I'm sorry! You're right, I just have SO much going on. Your suit looks so cute on you, Quinny! And the beard!" She stood up and put her arms out. "It is SO good to see you!"

Quinny approached Justine feeling like a lumbering moron and embraced her, fighting the urge to make it too intimate. She gave him a hard squeeze and broke away, holding him at arm's length and letting her eyes wander over his body and face.

"Oh my god!" she said, "You look so different! So scary! You're not a kid anymore! We gotta film a where-are-they-now for you when you've got something to promote. We'll call it *The Graveyard Stomper* and center it around your return to boxing. Maybe a T-shirt line or a craft beer. People love you; you know. I made a movie about these bull queer cops who have an LGTBQ fight club in Arkansas, and you were like a major celebrity to them."

"Jesus," he said, standing, shrugging his suit straight. "I mean, sounds good."

"Oh, before I forget," she said, placing a hand on his arm. "Where are you staying?

"I'll be over at the Marine Park Inn."

"Oh."

"Why?" he asked. "What's the problem?"

"It's just that I can't send Esme Camus to meet you at a place like that. Can you host her at your mom's house?"

"Mom's gone. Took off. Who the fuck is Esme Camus?"

"Didn't you have porn in prison?" she asked. "Esme's like the biggest alt-porn star in the world. She's a real-deal goth. You'll like her."

"And she wants to meet me?"

"Not really," she said. "I could find you a fangirl if you'd rather have that experience. Esme is a professional sex worker so please don't try to kiss her or go down on her like she's your girlfriend. She's not. She's my welcome home gift to you."

"Is she from one of your movies, too?"

"God, no. But you can order anything on an app now. Dinner, car service, porn stars. Why are you looking at me like that? There's not a man alive that doesn't watch porn. I was being nice!"

"I kind of thought we would . . ."

Justine's phone made a noise, and she was looking at it, wide-eyed. "Just give me one minute," she said, and turned around and settled back onto the sofa, her thumbs flying again.

Quinny turned and walked away. He didn't think she even noticed, but as he waited in front of the elevator, she called out, "Let's link up soon, okay? I meant what I said about the where-are-they-now film!"

That was somehow worse than if she'd just let him leave.

"Yeah, okay," he said.

Outside, he stripped off his jacket, tie, and shirt and walked to the Marine Park Inn in a white undershirt and brown dress pants, looking like an old drunk after a wedding.

CHAPTER TEN: GOTTA GO

At the Marine Park Inn, the same woman from the '90s was working the reception desk behind the bullet-proof glass. She had a beehive hairdo, blue eyeshadow, and smoked cigarettes like she didn't give a fuck. Her nametag said Myrna. *Well, that's perfect.*

"I spent so much money here when I was a kid living at my parents' house, I probably put the owner's kid through college," Quinny joked. "When you don't have anywhere else to bring a girl, that eleven bucks an hour adds up—am I right, Myrna?"

She didn't crack a smile. "Ya gotta tawk to Jakub about da room."

Her accent was so thick, he would have thought it was a put-on if he hadn't remembered her from his younger days. She took an exaggerated pause and gave him the thrice-over, her Virginia Slim dangling from her pink-stained lips.

"Yoo da boxuh?" she finally said.

He shrugged his shoulders.

"Good fuh you," Myrna said huskily. "Remembuh, you ain't a bounce-uh, live and let live, but when somethin's gotta get done, yuh gonna need tuh get yuh hands dirty."

It took all his self-control not to smirk or even break out laughing at this ridiculous scene and his absurd situation, but he clenched his jaw and nodded.

He sensed Jakub hovering behind him, then felt the man gingerly patting his shoulder. Quinny turned, keeping a serious expression, and had to keep fighting his smirk as he met Jakub's gaze. You'd think the kid was a Williamsburg hipster with his well-groomed, craft-brew-loving beard, large, feminine eyeglasses, and wiry build, but the yarmulke on his head told the real story.

"It's our honor to have you as our guest," Jakub said. His accent was vaguely Germanic. "Don't listen to Myrna. You're not going to be a night watchman here. That's just what I told my partner Modi so he wouldn't get jealous about you being around."

Quinny opened his mouth, then snapped it shut as he realized what was meant by "partner." He smiled and nodded.

"You can have the room as long as you need it," Jakub said. "Full cable package, Wi-Fi, a mini fridge, free heat and AC, and free breakfast every morning."

The "free breakfast" made Quinny unexpectedly happy. He hadn't realized how much he was worrying about just getting enough to eat. Awash in gratitude, he reached out for a handshake. Jakub went one further and came in for a close, chest-to-chest hug. Quinny felt himself tense up. He didn't have a problem with the gays—he met a few in the can—but he'd never hugged one before.

"People talk a big game," Jakub said as he eased out of the hug and looked Quinny square in the eye. "Every schmuck thinks they would punch a Nazi if they ever came across one, but you—you did it. This makes you a special person."

Quinny's mind blanked. He'd thought a million times of how that punch had ruined his life. He hoped Jakub couldn't see the conflict in his eyes.

It seemed that he didn't. He dropped the volume of his voice, trying to sound tough. "However, if I need you, you'll be available for me, won't you?"

"Sure thing, boss," Quinny mumbled, startled to hear himself sounding like some Hollywood thug talking to a criminal mastermind, wondering how this fucker got him to forget his dignity and play this part.

"Good boy," Jakub said, obviously pleased with Quinny's attitude.

"So, this ain't a security job," Quinny said bluntly. "It's muscle work."

Jakub raised his professionally shaped eyebrows and gave Quinny a big grin. Quinny wasn't sure how much of an upgrade this new situation would turn out to be, but at least he wasn't gonna be sleeping in a truck parked in a junkyard.

CHAPTER ELEVEN: FIGHT THE REAL ENEMY

To get to Scruffy Murphy's, Quinny had to take the Kings Highway bus to Bath Avenue, then transfer to another bus to Bay Ridge. He felt good being out in the world. It was a sunny day, and Southern Brooklyn was bustling. Nothing much seemed to have changed, except girls now wore leggings as pants, which he counted as a plus, and everyone seemed to stare at their phones all the time. After he saw one, two, five, eight seemingly sane people casually talking to themselves, he started to think that schizophrenia had gone mainstream. Then it dawned on him that these people were wearing wireless headphones, connected to their cells, and he laughed at his own stupidity.

It wasn't like he was unaware of the smartphone revolution. On the inside, he had a vague sense of developments out in the world, but the fact was that, although some inmates had smartphones, he hadn't ever used one. He didn't have anyone to call, and he didn't need to watch the Mets in the World Series bad enough to owe some con a favor for letting him hold their ass-smuggled Android.

As he traveled, Quinny found himself marveling at how much he'd missed, but he was surprised to note that he wasn't bothered by that fact. His good mood held until Scruffy Murphy's came into view. The place was a corny, prefab

Irish pub located next to the Social Security office on Fourth Avenue. A drunk patron slouched outside, next to the door, looking like he resented the sun's glare. The man was unshaven and twitching, looking up and down the street, waiting for someone. Quinny nodded at him as he pushed the heavy, dark door open. The man nodded back.

Although he'd never been in the place, it was eerily familiar as Quinny walked in and climbed aboard a barstool. Nineties alternative music played on the sound system. Shady figures lurked in the back. The clientele was made up of guys who binged after their checks came on the first and fifteenth, and red-faced off-the-boaters who went through hell to get here but drank away their second chances. A sign behind the bar advertised a two-for-one Smithwick's special and by the look—and smell—of things, the man seated next to Quinny at the bar must have downed thirty of the red ales.

Not only did the guy look like an unmade bed—maybe fifty, sixty years old, wearing stained jeans and a rumpled flannel shirt—but anyone with a nose could tell he'd shit himself. Quinny ordered and raised his eyebrows when his pints were set before him. The bartender muttered, "I already asked him to leave, but Old McShitpants won't budge until he finishes his pints."

"Fair play to him," croaked the whiskey pickle sitting to the other side of Quinny. Quinny glanced over. The man's swollen pink nose looked like a brain.

McShitpants might be a stroke of luck. A half-assed wiseguy like Tony Dukes, if he was around, wouldn't be able to resist getting in the middle of things if a situation came up. Any opportunity to be the big man. Quinny sat back and let the scene play out with the two pints of ale in front of him.

After a couple of minutes, as if he'd made it happen with psychic power, Quinny saw a figure stand up from one of the booths in the back of the bar. It was a short guy with coiffed gray hair wearing a black satin jacket that doubtlessly had a logo on the back for a dart league or softball team or some bullshit like that. The guy brushed off his pant legs, adjusted his expression, and squinted at McShitpants. *Tony LoDuca*, Quinny thought as he watched the man saunter up the path between booths and bar. Quinny remembered LoDuca as somewhat impressive, but it had been a hell of a long time. The man tried to look like John Gotti, and he did—if Gotti was actually the plumbing supply salesman he professed to be.

Quinny leaned back and polished off his first pint as Tony Dukes approached McShitpants. He felt pissed at Bartley for getting robbed by this little cartoon character. Dukes made a disgusted face as he got close enough to smell the bum. "It's time to go, buddy," he said.

"You need a hand with this guy?" Quinny asked.

Dukes looked over and Quinny knew the mobster recognized him. "I'd appreciate it," Dukes said.

Quinny slid off his stool and grabbed McShitpants by the collar, holding his breath as he did so. The drunk slurred, "Hey, pal!" and squirmed, knocking over his empty pint glass, but he felt as frail and light as a ninety-year-old woman. A barfly moved ahead and pulled the door open as Quinny stood the man up and led him across the floor. The drunk muttered, but stumbled into the daylight, and the door shut behind him. When Quinny turned around, brushing his hands against each other, he received a round of applause from a few of the patrons and a nod from Tony Dukes. The mobster pointed to two more Smithwick's, which he'd ordered for Quinny. "Welcome home, champ," he said, extending a hand.

Quinny didn't want to shake, but it was part of what he'd come to do. Tony Dukes squeezed hard, glanced at a couple of the drinkers, and said, "Jesus, this kid's hand is the size of a canned ham. No wonder he creamed that eggplant and won the Golden Gloves."

"I'm surprised you remember," Quinny said.

"Consider me a fan," Dukes said. "It's not every day a kid from the neighborhood wins the Gloves, then kills a man with his bare hands. I still got the back page of the *Post* with the headline 'He's White and He Can Fight' taped up in my office."

Dukes motioned for the bartender to bring Quinny's now-three pints into his private booth. They sat across from each other. Quinny felt gigantic looking down at the small, middle-aged Italian.

"Do you remember me?" Dukes said.

Quinny nodded. "I know exactly who you are. That's why I'm here. You know my dad . . ."

Dukes gave Quinny a sympathetic look, then peered off to the side. "Real fucking shame about how things turned out with him."

"What's that supposed to mean?"

Dukes looked Quinny in the eye. "Your old man drank his whole life away when you were inside. Lost your mother, the business, the house—and his fucking mind. The guy's out there in the street telling everybody I owe him forty Gs. That's why you're here, right? Come on, kid, if that was true, and I was burning people when they won, who'd lay a bet with me? How would I stay in business? Junkman Quinn couldn't handle losing everything like that. He needed somebody to blame."

"My father," Quinny said, "is no fucking liar."

"And I ain't a deadbeat," Dukes said.

They stared each other down for several seconds.

"Look," Dukes finally said, "I understand how you feel. It's your old man. I'd be doing just what you're doing if I was in your shoes. I'm just telling you how it really is."

Quinny could think of nothing to say. Dukes took advantage of his silence:

"To kinda smooth things over, how'd you like to make seven hundred fifty bucks tonight?"

They stared each other down again. Quinny wanted to tell this little weasel to get fucked but could already feel the cash in his pocket. "Make seven hundred fifty bucks how?" he finally said.

"Jimmy, it's the easiest money you'll ever make," Dukes said. "This guy's breaking his contract, not coming up with what he legitimately owes. He's a stockbroker, for Chrissake. He gets one look at you, he'll probably hand you the money and ask for a photo together for his Instagram. And get this—the guy's some kind of swinger. The wife's unbelievable looking. The ripest tomato you ever seen. She's a real good time, from what I hear. Maybe a bonus in it for you."

Quinny felt his cock stiffening at the last statement, which made him feel even shittier. The guy he'd come to straighten out had not only taken control of the situation, but he also had Quinny putting the squeeze on some other poor SOB, who was probably getting screwed as bad as Bartley.

But what did he care about some stockbroker? He thought of the seven fifty again and heard himself say, "All right."

Dukes looked like he was trying not to grin. He raised his pint. "You're a good man, Jimmy. Here's to your success on the outside."

Quinny nodded, raised his own glass, and drank.

CHAPTER TWELVE: SOMEBODY'S GONNA GET THEIR HEAD KICKED IN TONIGHT

Jordan Rinaldi was a hedge-fund bullshit artist at a company called Crowley Capital. He'd bought three units in a new-construction glass-tower luxury building in Sheepshead Bay, tore the walls down, and made one giant condo. That's all Quinny knew about the guy. That and he didn't like the looks of the dude from the picture Tony Dukes pulled up on his phone. Rinaldi had an orange tan and a little boy's haircut—clipped and combed forward like Julius fucking Caesar.

It was four or five when Quinny knocked on Rinaldi's door. He was still a little buzzed, and still pissed about doing this. His instructions were to pick up seventy-five hundred bucks, which should be ready to go in an envelope. Then he had to make his way to Jack's Joint, the doo-wop record shop that Greaser Jack still ran over on East Thirty-Sixth and Flatlands Ave. He'd find Dukes there.

He was looking forward to seeing the old mobster after twenty years, but something about Greaser Jack backing Dukes didn't sit right. Quinny sensed a trap, but he couldn't figure the angle. Today he just wanted to get this shit over with, get his ten percent, and get clear.

Rinaldi was shirtless when he opened the door. The guy was average sized, maybe he'd lifted in college, but those days were long gone. He was flabby and sweating like he'd been digging a ditch, with dark strands of brown hair sticking to his forehead. His torso was almost completely hairless. His coked-out eyes darted every which way. Instead of looking at Quinny's face, they fixed on his right hand. Quinny followed the man's gaze and marveled at his own mitt for a moment. It was gnarled from so many breaks Quinny lost count, and the veins stood out almost obscenely. Traces of the Viva Hate tattoo Justine gave him all those years ago were still visible on the backs of the fingers.

Keep staring, asshole, I might do a trick.

"Mr. Quinn," Rinaldi said, licking his lips. "I know why you're here. Listen—"

"Aren't you going to invite me in?" Quinny said. "Offer me a glass of water? I'm thirsty."

"Look, Quinn, about the money, the thing is—"

Quinny stepped over the threshold, forcing Rinaldi to back out of his way, and kicked the door shut behind him. *Holy fucking Saturday Night Fever*, he thought, glancing around the apartment's interior. The walls were completely mirrored, the floors were marble, and the furniture was made of black Formica that even Quinny knew was tacky.

"I can give you three grand today," Rinaldi said. His voice was weak. "I make deals like this all the time. I'm a businessman. Look, I've got a deal for you. Hear me out, will ya?"

Quinny felt his temper rising. "Just hand over the full amount," he said, "and we can keep this party polite."

"I wish it was that easy!" Rinaldi said, blinking spasmodically, sweat glistening on his upper lip. "Listen, I'll give you the three grand I have in cash now, and I'll give you three times that—nine grand in cash—two weeks from today."

Quinny stepped closer, and Rinaldi stepped back, but kept talking. "I'm not looking to get pinched for insider trading," he blurted, "but I can tell you, right? I'm waiting on this company PSYC to hit. It's a penny stock. Do you know what that is? When LSD and shrooms become medicinally and recreationally legal like weed, this stock is gonna blast off and I'm sitting on millions and millions of shares. Believe me, this is the future of medicine. Two weeks from now, I'll triple your investment. Nine grand in your hand."

Rinaldi seemed to become aware as he said the last word, and glanced at Quinny's right hand again, which was now coming toward his face. The hedge-funder took the punch in his eye socket and stumbled backward. Quinny stepped toward him, backing him up to one of the black tables. "Guys like you are unbelievable," he said, feeling his anger break through. "Your fucking dining room table probably cost twenty grand and you can't cough up seventy-five hundred?"

He slapped Rinaldi in the temple. The man went down and immediately began crawling away. Quinny bent and took a handful of greasy hair and wrenched Rinaldi's head backward.

He really didn't want to do this, but he wasn't about to go back forty-five-hundred short to cover a coke fiend with a fugazi pump-and-dump scheme. On the other hand, if he gave Dukes three grand and a photo of Rinaldi's busted face, he'd get the two weeks leeway and pocket the extra cash. Plus, he wouldn't lose his standing with the gangster.

That, he decided, was what he had to do.

Rinaldi seemed to be reading his thoughts. "Listen," the slimy fuck said, with his eyes rolling up to meet Quinny's, either unaware of, or unconcerned about, how pathetic he looked. "I'll sweeten the deal! You front me the money. I pay you back ten grand, transfer two thousand shares of PSYC, and, oh fuck, sonofa . . . goddammit . . ." He twisted his skinnyfat body to keep his neck from breaking as Quinny lifted him by the hair. "*You get to fuck my wife!*" he said. "*Do anything you want with her—she takes it any way you like!*"

Quinny felt his cock stiffening again. *Goddammit.*

"*Regina! Regina!*" Rinaldi yelled; his voice hoarse. "*Get out here! Right now!*"

Holding a limp Jordan Rinaldi off the ground by the hair, Quinny looked up. He heard heavy heels echo on the tiles, and watched as the woman came around the corner, hit sideways by the sconce lighting, shaded like a scene in an old porno.

Holy fuck.

She was hot. Too hot for this guy. Her face was a beautiful mask made from layers of makeup, giant fake eyelashes, and lip and cheek injections. She had wild black curls and a tanned, toned body whose sculpted abs and obliques were exposed by a brief, strappy bra top. The tits were convincing, though he guessed they were bought and paid for. As she stepped toward him her thighs were too shapely, unreal in her black, painted-on yoga pants.

Quinny realized now that this was a setup. A gift from Dukes. He knew he was being played somehow. But why not take what he was offered?

Regina shot her husband a look, then locked eyes with Quinny and held out her hand. Her come-hither expression was as sincere as any porn queen's. Quinny shoved Rinaldi's head toward the floor and stood up straight, feeling the strain in his jeans. He stepped over the slimeball's legs and allowed himself to be led through the sprawling living room, around a corner, down a hallway, and into the bedroom.

The *Saturday Night Fever* motif repeated in here with mirrored walls, black end tables, and a king-sized bed. Regina stopped in front of the bed, turned around, dropped to her knees on a white shag rug, and pulled Quinny over by the waist of his pants. She quickly got his jeans open, pulled his cock out, and dove in—over-the-top porno style with gagging, slobbering, the works, getting him fully hard. Part of him was furious, because after two decades of dreaming about shit that wasn't half this good, he couldn't fully concentrate. He looked, instinctively, to the open door of the room, and there was Rinaldi, peeking around the corner, probably yanking himself out of view.

"What the fuck!" Quinny said, and shoved Regina's head but her lips did not dislodge. "Get the fuck out of here!"

Regina clung to his belt loops, and her voice came to him in a stage whisper. "I hate him. He's a loser. He ruined my life. I want him to watch a real man fuck me! Come on!" She pulled him toward the bed. Quinny laughed. He was starting to like Regina. *Sure. Why not give her a thrill?* It wasn't until later that he realized she'd said this for Rinaldi's sake, not his.

He glanced over his shoulder and didn't see Rinaldi, but he could sense the guy there. He had half a mind to rush into the hall and run the fucker off, but Regina shook her head discreetly when he turned back and was now stripped out of her top. She bent, peeling off her yoga pants, and her ass was like a heart as she crawled onto the bed. Quinny felt like his breath had been knocked out of him. *Since when did Italian girls have asses like that?* She posed on all fours, inviting him, looking back at him. He tore his fly open all the way and clumsily went for it. Her skin was smooth and soft, she smelled like lavender and roses, and she was absolutely drenched.

He hit it from behind, raw. She bucked like a rodeo bronco and took control. If Quinny thought about what was happening or allowed himself to be in the moment and feel the sensation, he'd have come in ten seconds. He didn't want to be a ten-pump chump. He tried to distract himself, and his thoughts landed again on Jordan Rinaldi, and why this was even happening. That killed the vibe for him. Now he looked down on her, and her act was as fake as her tits. She was screaming and wailing like she was being split in two, but he was only half hard. He didn't want to cheat himself out of the payoff, and he tried to find something in his memory bank to bring his mojo back . . . but it was too late. Now he was thinking about the hedge-fund weasel right around the corner, and he wondered if these two degenerates had any kids.

The last thought killed it completely. He flopped out of her, stuffed his cock into place and zipped. He suddenly wanted the fuck out of there. "What's wrong, honey?" Regina said, but he'd already turned away. When he exited the bedroom, he practically knocked Rinaldi over. The guy was zipping up his slacks. "We're cool, right?" he stammered, his eyes wide. "I told you she'd do whatever you wanted, right?" He put out a hand to shake.

"Fuck you," Quinny said, seizing the hand, feeling it turn to putty as he squeezed. He yanked the arm and swung his head down, slamming the bridge of Rinaldi's nose with his forehead.

Quinny opened his hand and Rinaldi went stumbling backward, holding his face, bleating like a fucking goat into his palms. Quinny pulled his phone from his back pocket and thumbed the camera icon. "Let's see your face, shithead," he said. Rinaldi lowered his hands. His eyes were streaming tears, and his nose streaming blood, spots of it landing on the tiles, and marking his flabby chest and stomach. Quinny snapped the picture.

"You didn't have to do that!" Regina said from the bedroom doorway. She was wearing a pink robe now, with fake fur around the collar. He looked her up and down, feeling disgust along with his unsatisfied lust.

"I think he likes it," Quinny said, looking back at Rinaldi. "And unless he wants more of the same, he's going to come up with the three grand he mentioned, and I'll see if I can buy him some time."

CHAPTER THIRTEEN: BROOKLYN BASTARDS

The next morning, Quinny was awoken by a loud, incessant honking noise in the parking lot of the motel. He heaved himself out of bed and peered through the blinds to find Tommy Reardon waiting outside like a stalker. Sitting on a shit box Toyota Camry, he looked like a kid waiting for his friend to come out and play stickball. He wore black slacks with a Motörhead T-shirt and a sport coat. It wasn't hip and it wasn't businesslike, but on him, it seemed right. Tommy double-fisted large black coffees in Anthora Greek-style paper cups that said, "We are happy to serve you." *One of those better be for me.*

"You don't lose your virginity to trucker coffee," Tommy said. "You build up to it. Just like you don't bench press three hundred pounds on your first day at the gym. You gotta build a foundation."

"What the fuck are you talking about?" Quinny looked annoyed.

"I have like five or six of these things a day, helps me power through anything," Tommy said. "It's a large Café Bustelo from the bodega and the guy puts in a scoop of something called Diesel Energy. Puts two sometimes."

"That's speed," Quinny said. "Meth. German fighter pilot juice."

Tommy smiled and tapped himself on the head. "If that's the case, I get why people like it. I get more done in a morning than most people do in a week. My brain power exponentially expands. I'm seventeen moves ahead of the next guy. A third scoop and I'll take over the world."

He didn't seem to be joking. He didn't seem to be wrong, either.

Quinny knew that Tommy loved him more than his own family. When they met, Tommy was a nerdy kid who would have been just another victim if Quinny, Carlos, and the Graveyard Stompers didn't look out for him in school. Tommy appreciated their intervention and didn't forget, even after he made it big in finance—that's rare. Usually, people tried to put space between themselves and the Graveyard Stompers, especially when it involved Quinny. Tommy was a silent partner in Carlos's bars and clubs, he bailed Joe Damage out of an underwater mortgage, and made sure Quinny's prison commissary account was always topped up.
Back in the joint, Quinny thought fondly of Tommy every time he slurped down ramen noodles with jack mackerel on his bunk. Sometimes he used those funds to buy Vaseline to jack off with. He filled a toilet paper tube with the stuff and wrapped it in an old sock to make a fifi. He tried not to think of Tommy then. *You do what you gotta do to get by on the inside.*

When Quinny was in prison, he cut himself off from everyone. Any weirdness between them was entirely his fault. Tommy did everything he could to hook him up at first, but he didn't want people to see him weak and at the mercy of that bullshit institution. *Pure ego.* But when things went to shit and Quinny ended up in protective custody—a nice way of saying isolation—he regretted it.

At one point, he was so desperate for human contact that he would have consented to a visit from the cop whose kid he killed. Even if the officer yelled and berated him, at least he'd be acknowledged by another human being. Quinny spent so much time in his head, he had started to question if he was still a person. The only one he could've tolerated seeing face-to-face was Justine—he even put her on the list of approved visitors just in case, but she never showed.

Tommy was never slow on his feet, but now he moved like he was trying to win an Olympic gold medal in speed walking. "Keep up," he shouted from ahead. "We're going on a tour of the old neighborhood."

Tommy seemed genuinely excited, like he had this planned for two decades. Quinny caught up to his old friend and set eyes on those familiar streets in daylight for the first time in a very long time.

Marine Park had a complete overhaul. It actually looked pleasant: lush and green, with organized areas for sports and activities, like a park you'd see out in the suburbs of Jersey or Long Island. Nothing like the shit heap it used to be. The playground was crowded with children and their parents, who hovered close as they ran through sprinklers and nervously climbed monkey bars. The idea that these parents wasted a day off watching their brats dick around on the monkey bars instead of chugging Jim Beam until they blacked out—it was downright sweet.

His own parents fed and bathed him, but what he did from morning until dinnertime wasn't their problem. He wasn't alone—in the '80s, the neighborhood kids were feral. Maybe not raised-by-wolves feral, but close. *Maybe these kids will turn out better. Either that or they'll be soft veal calves. Odds are about fifty-fifty on that.*

The park was a "melting pot" in a neighborhood where no one believed diversity was their strength. It was set up a lot like prison. Segregated.

Men from the West Indies still played cricket in impossibly clean white sweaters. Off-the-boat Italians and Irish still played soccer with Russians and Latinos. They formed teams by homeland and had professional-looking jerseys made like they were competing in the Construction Workers' World Cup. Bartley pushed his son to play for the Brooklyn Shamrocks like he had, but Quinny told him that soccer was "gay" and "for homos." During his time in the can, he learned those words didn't go over too well on the outside anymore, so he wouldn't say it that way today. But he still thought soccer was stupid. For Chrissake, he was an American.

All the friends he and Tommy drank forties of malt liquor with and all the kids they fought before Brooklyn got civilized—where were they now? Quinny scanned Marine Park and asked, "Is MPB still around?"

Tommy snorted. "Were the Marine Park Boys ever really around? It was just the Florio brothers and a bunch of dead weight. I never rated them as a crew."

The Florios were Marine Park royalty: four brothers who loved to fight and were damn good at it—easily the toughest kids in the neighborhood.

"I'd rather four berserker Florios have my back than ten human beings. Shit, I'd take the Florio boys and their sister over most armies," Quinny said. "Once they got going, those guys never stopped fighting. Nice guys when they weren't biting somebody's ear off. What the hell are they up to?"

"On the straight and narrow," Tommy said. "They're all upstanding citizens now if you can believe it. Solid family men with real jobs, mortgages, 401Ks—the whole nine. Still see them around from time to time, and I'm pretty sure they could still form up like Voltron to straighten out any neighborhood beefs if they had to. They might be even more dangerous now. They all know jiu jitsu."

This was the kind of news Quinny wanted to hear.

As they walked toward Midwood, the landscape was both similar and different than he'd remembered. A Jewish bar called Cafe Hadar replaced The King's Castle, the old mob front where his father used to drink, play cards, and bet on European soccer. There were still some signs up in Russian, but they were outnumbered by those in Hebrew and something that looked vaguely Chinese. He was genuinely excited when he noticed Quentin Pizza was still there.

They popped in to get a slice. The old owner Jerry had sold the place to Pedro and Sixto, the Mexican guys who made the pizza when he got too arthritic to do it himself. Their pies tasted better, and they added tacos and tortas to the menu—a massive improvement. Sitting at the plastic table with a fistful of paper napkins, Tommy used his other hand to lift his slice, and took a massive bite.

"Fuck Per Se," he said. "I've had tasting menus at six of the top ten restaurants in the world, and nothing beats a slice of greasy Brooklyn pizza and a too-syrupy fountain Coke." Quinny missed this. He knew it was cliché, but he missed crunchy-on-the-outside, soft-on-the-inside bagels from Brooklyn Bagel, loaded kebabs from Sahara on Coney Island Avenue, potato knishes down on Brighton Beach. He missed obnoxious kids playing street hockey, cantankerous senior citizens setting up beach chairs on the sidewalk in the summer because they didn't have air conditioning, even Guido cars with a presidential tint aggressively pumping freestyle music. Already today he'd heard "Spring Love" by Stevie B and Taylor Dayne's "Tell it to My Heart."

Being back flooded Quinny's mind with memories. He thought about the Quentin Road

Boys hanging out on this block when he was a kid and how much he wanted to be a tough graffiti writer like those guys. Back in the day, they'd relieve themselves in a designated piss corner in the PS 222 schoolyard. Miss Reagan's fifth grade class had to line up every morning, standing in dried piss and inhaling the stink. Hilarious until Quinny was in Miss Reagan's fifth grade class.

He asked Tommy, "What happened to QRB? I don't see any graffiti."

"Heroin happened," Tommy said. He stopped in his tracks and started picking at his cuticle. "The guys a little older than you, they're all gone. I should have gotten my hands on a yearbook. Almost everyone you went to school with, Quinny. You'll see. Mostly opioids and suicide. I'm sorry, bro."

Maybe being sent to prison was a blessing. Maybe a cage was the safest place for me this whole time. Nah. Fuck that.

"Alex Vostoff is dead? What about that kid Mario?" Quinny asked. "Matt Connors? Brandon Schwartz?"

"They found Alex in the alleyway that leads to the schoolyard and said it was 'natural causes' but everyone knows that's bullshit. Mario Suarez OD'd in a welfare hotel and some sick fucks put a video of it on the internet. Matt crashed his car into a family and wiped them all out. He drove home and ate a gun. Couldn't live with the guilt. Schwartz had shit for lungs after 9/11, swallowed a bottle of Xanax and washed it down with a bottle of Jack. He took himself out before the cancer did. For a while, the newspapers were calling it 'death by despair.' Some of the neighborhood moms buried two, three sons. Poor old ladies. What can you do?"

Quinny pretended to be moved, but he realized he didn't actually give a shit.

They passed by the old Quinn house. It wasn't red brick anymore. The new owners refaced it in white. It looked a lot nicer.

He didn't want to linger with ghosts too long, so they kept moving. After making a left onto Kings Highway, he felt nostalgia take over. Hasidic Jews still brazenly triple-parked without fear of getting a ticket. Nobody knew why the cops never wrote them tickets, but they straight up didn't. The Orthodox families had upgraded from station wagons to SUVs, but they still sped down the street menacing pedestrians like it was a game of *Frogger*. (The exception was Friday nights and Saturdays when the holy rollers weren't allowed to drive.)

"Accidents in the city must go down eighty percent when the Brooklyn Cowboys are off the road," Tommy joked.

Finally, Quinny spotted some familiar faces—the Kings Highway Boys. They looked like Kings Highway Middle-Aged Men now: bloated, balding, facial hair streaked with gray. They were still selling rocks, pills, and Charlie in front of Highway Bagels. Tommy said this was their backup location, so cops must be watching their usual dope spot near the train station. The scene was an unsettling mix of past and present: on the wrong side of forty, slinging the exact same drugs, wearing the exact same baggy Carhartt jeans and Timberland boots they did back in the '90s.

Quinny made the mistake of returning ROLO's head nod and mumbling, "What's up?" He didn't know the guy's real name, only his graffiti tag. Quinny imagined ROLO living in his mom's basement, stealing her pain meds, and just waiting it out. Once she dropped dead, he'd inherit the house and turn it into a full-on crack den.

Quinny knew he had to walk over and shake hands. Him and Tommy wanted to bounce as quickly as they could without being rude. A guy called Anton he vaguely remembered kept asking Quinny to go with him to the Sixty-Third Precinct to try to get his "property" back. The cops stole it, Anton said, and since Quinny was kinda famous, maybe it would miraculously appear.

"I don't think so, bro," Quinny said, shaking his head and walking away. "I killed a cop's kid, remember?"

Anton said, "Oh, shit, my bad," fifty or sixty times.

After dipping out of that conversation, they walked toward the train station. Quinny asked about going downtown and hitting St. Mark's Place to run into punks and hardcore kids. He wanted lunch at Dojo. The $3.95 soy patty special was something he dreamed about while he was away. It was a ridiculously filling lump of battered and fried tofu, slathered in carrot-ginger dressing served over brown rice. That calorie bomb saved his ass when he was near broke so many times. It was also the place he brought girls on dates. It came with a side salad. *Classy.* Tommy gave him an exaggerated, wide-eyed look.

"Damn, it really has been a long time," Tommy said. "Dojo's gone. St. Mark's has been dead for at least ten years. All of downtown is one giant cafeteria for NYU students now. If you're looking for punk and hardcore, look at old pictures or make friends with millennials in Bushwick. What's there now ain't the East Village you remember."

He gave a puzzled look.

"Look, Quinny," Tommy said, "time doesn't stand still. The Lower East Side isn't a museum dedicated to your youth. CBGB is gone. And you know what? Before it closed, they put on shitty shows for a decade. Continental closed. The Wetlands is gone. Limelight's gone. It's a fucking exercise studio now. The artists and freaks moved to Portland or Detroit or New Orleans. It's a different world. All the kids now are herbs. They ride exercise bikes, eat plant-based food, watch *Friends,* and post pictures of their asses online instead of living life."

"Jeez, Tommy," he said, "you're depressing the fuck out of me with all this. Can we at least get roast beef sandwiches at Brennan and Carr, or have they turned it into a yoga studio yet?"

"Still there," Tommy said excitedly, "but the guy who made their rolls died ten years ago. The new bread's just not the same. It doesn't soak up the beef broth when you dip it like the old one did. It's like a rock. Believe it or not, Roll N' Roaster has the best roast beef sandwich in Brooklyn these days. Better than John's Deli in Bensonhurst. They use Franco-American gravy and treat you like an asshole."

"Ha! I'm used to that," said Quinny. "But wait, what's up with the hardcore crews?"

"I don't know what to tell you. They're not really a thing anymore. I mean, DMS is still DMS. The OGs are still holding it down. But the new kids are different than we were. They're well adjusted. They want to save the world. Their bands are incredible. Mindforce, Age of Apocalypse, and Zulu are everything we wanted out of a hardcore band when we were 16. Even The Superbowl of Hardcore had to change its name under threat of lawsuit from the NFL. It's called the Black N Blue Bowl now, and every band that ever existed plays at it. Newjacks, old heads; they get everybody to play. Sick shows, though. People fly in from all over the world, bring their kids, and make a hardcore vacation of it. Every band from the '80s and '90s reunited—even Judge—got put on the bill."

"Damn," he said, "I never got a chance to see Judge. I wore their New York Crew shirt with the crossed hammers so often it burned out, then I gave it to you. They broke up right before I started to go to shows."

"The first two reunion shows were mind blowing. Then they hung around too long."

"The Brooklyn Boot Boys are all cops and firemen now," Tommy continued. "Republicans. They still go to shows, but they spend more time talking about politics and conspiracy theories than they do music. A lot of the tough old heads became weirdo right wingers or crazy commies. They still fight, but now they're called Antifa and the Proud Boys. They're gonna both try to claim you as theirs with your extensive background in Nazi punching."

Quinny shook his head in disbelief. "They can keep that bullshit. What about the Graveyard Stompers? Anybody carry on our legacy?"

"Nah," Tommy said. "The whole crew folded when your drama happened. The news said we were a gang; cops were on our asses. We had to shut it all down. Not a lot of happy endings with the Brooklyn hardcore crews. Skinhead Carlos is good, though. He married a model, the son of a bitch, and he lives in Jersey like a regular guy. Joe Damage sells real estate and Vinny Dago is a captain in the fire department. After 9/11, Cyrus got religious and stopped talking to the rest of us."

"Oof," Quinny said. "Well, I saw Justine for five seconds last night. Wasn't impressed. When I was inside all I cared about—all that kept me going—was the hope of finding Justine on Facebook and getting my mom to make me a steak smothered with mushrooms and onions when I got out. Disappointed on both fronts."

"I figured you'd be on that mission," Tommy said. "She's not one of us anymore. Justine's a major documentary filmmaker now, a huge fucking deal. Awards. Premieres. Hair and makeup people. She dated Michael Fassbender for a minute."

"Who?" Quinny asked.

"You don't know him. The point is, she did something to her face and now she's actually smoking hot. Still nuts, though."

"She was the zookeeper, and we were the animals," Quinny gritted his teeth. "She made her bones with *Nazi Killer*. Now she's got a dope apartment and fancy French awards and I wasted twenty years in a cell. We're not square."

"I know, I know." Tommy deeply exhaled from the back of his throat. "She's done a lot since then. There was a movie about Bedouin nomads smuggling drugs and Russian sex workers into Israel from Egypt. That shit was crazy—she let them wrap her up in a rug and rode on a camel all night through the desert."

"Still though, you think they'd let her make that movie if the one about us didn't blow up? We made her famous."

"She became everything she said she would. I'm just saying, she's big time. If you're gonna pursue Justine, you can't just be prison swole, talking about back in the day. You need to come correct. What are you gonna do to impress a woman who's seen it all and caught it on film?"

“She doesn’t give a fuck about me,” Quinny said. “But she wants to use me for another movie.”

CHAPTER FOURTEEN: GUESS I GOTTA LEARN THE HARD WAY AGAIN

Quinny dutifully walked to the appointed drop-off location. Jack's Joint was the last remaining doo-wop record store in New York City. Rows and rows of old vinyl records and stacks of forty-fives. Pictures of a younger Greaser Jack with legends like Frankie Lymon and Dion DiMucci adorned the walls.

Who the hell shopped at a doo-wop record store in this day and age? Nobody. And that was the point.

An ancient turntable played an original vinyl record, the voice of Randy Leeds bellowing "*My Oh My*" at high volume. Greaser Jack sat behind the counter looking like a seventy-year-old teenager from 1957, with a vintage blue sharkskin jacket and his switchblade pompadour now gone shock-white. He still looked vital, despite the wrinkles and white hair, and it gave Quinny a good feeling.

Jack was a proper gangster. Last of an all-but-dead breed. No casting director in Hollywood could find a better boss. He looked up and froze. Jack didn't take his eyes off Quinny as the ex-con approached the counter. He reached down and turned a knob, so Randy Leeds and his band became a much smaller presence.

Jack extended his hand to shake but, in a last-minute swerve, Quinny leaned over the counter to hug the old guy.

"Quinny," he said, "it's about fucking time you come by, no? I gotta hear through the grapevine that Dukes has you doing Mickey Mouse jobs? You're living in the *putanna* hotel? How do you think that makes me look?"

Quinny tried to answer, but tripped on his words, "Jack, I—"

Jack dismissed his attempt to speak with a glare and continued. "It looks like I can't take care of you on the outside. Just like I couldn't keep you out of static on the inside. Quinny, you gotta stop acting like a maniac; it's making me look bad in the street."

"Jack," he said, "I didn't want to come to you for a favor. I wanted to come here on my own two feet to visit an old friend, not as a guy with his hand out."

"I know five hundred guys, easy," Jack said, "and none of them are good at anything except for you with the fighting. That's it. Everybody else is a bum and a do-nothing. And you threw it all away to be the boxing champ of the big house."

Jack's face reddened; spittle gathered at the corners of his mouth. His voice grew grave. "You didn't have to fight every Monday who broke your balls inside," he said.

Quinny looked at him quizzically. "Monday?"

"Kid," he said, "nobody likes Mondays. Think about it." Jack ran one hand over the other to indicate skin color. He laughed at his own joke, but Quinny stiff-necked him.

"You got it all wrong, Jack," Quinny said. "It was guys who looked like us that gutted me. I made the mistake of letting my guard down. Never again."

"You coulda been out years ago and retired by now. Instead, I gotta figure out how to milk the pro debut of a thirty-eight-year-old fighter with no professional record. You cost us both a lot of money."

Quinny narrowed his eyes at the old Italian. "Milk *what*?"

"Listen," Jack said, "I don't know anything about the bullshit with your old man and Dukes. Nobody ever came to me. But I don't like you breaking legs for fucking peanuts. You deserve better. And I can get you better."

Quinny swallowed. "What's the deal, Jack?"

"How would you like to make a hundred large to fight a washed-up ex-UFC champ in bareknuckle boxing?"

Quinny stared at the old man. He thought of the endless beatings he'd given—and taken—inside, for nothing. For less than nothing . . . "Fuck, Jack," he said. "I don't know what to say. That kind of money would . . . Look, whatever I need to do, it's done."

"You can say thank you for starters. Anyway, it's two hundred grand, but it goes half to me as promoter and manager, half to you. An easy hundred large in your pocket. Gets you back on your feet and in the public eye."

Quinny nodded, trying to process. "This UFC guy any good?"

"Nah, he's a garbage bag," Jack said. "None of these MMA guys can box for shit. Guy's name is Roman Kashan. Look him up. He lost his last three fights. A stiff breeze knocks him over."

"I can't thank you enough for this. I mean that. I can help out the old man because of this. Forget Dukes. I'll straighten him out another time."

"Here's the catch: The wheels are already in motion. You only got three weeks to get in fighting shape. The guy Kashan is set to fight is gonna bust a rib in camp, and you're gonna step in. The Nazi Killer is gonna be a bigger draw than the big chooch we had him matched up with. The thing's gonna be on streaming pay per view from an Indian reservation in Florida. If your old man isn't up for training you, go see Heather Hardy down at Gleason's. She's a helluva trainer."

Jack put his hands on Quinny's shoulders and looked him square in the face. "Now do me a favor. Quit trying to be a gangster and go be a fighter. Time ain't on your side and neither is luck."

Quinny held the old mobster's gaze.

After a moment, Jack sighed loudly, patted Quinny's shoulder and ended the moment. "Tony's in the back." Jack nodded his head toward a door beyond the counter. "Do your business with him and tell him what I got lined up for you, and that you ain't gonna be working for him no more."

Quinny nodded, trying to clear his head, trying not to think about the hundred grand. He patted his back pocket where the envelope was and strode toward the door. He rapped three times. After half a minute or so it was pulled open by a hulking young mook. Quinny entered, and looked at the guy, who was pushing the door shut. He figured six foot seven, probably three hundred pounds. The mook gave him a scowl and Quinny smirked. He'd put big fuckers like this on ice more than once. They always overestimate themselves.

His eyes stung from the smoke in the air. Five wise guys sat around an antique poker table, playing cards and gnawing on cigars. They wore Members Only jackets and dress slacks. A hazy, lentil-shaped cloud hung over the group, like the cloud in pictures of Mt. Fuji. Dukes was on the far side of the table. He looked up and smiled at Quinny and took the cigar from his mouth. "The man of the hour!" he said, yelling to be heard over the TV, which was playing one of those court programs, cranked to high volume for the old men.

The mook stepped over and sat at a different card table, before a half-eaten hero sandwich, keeping an eye on Quinny as he chewed.

The other old men straightened their backs, lowered their cards, and looked at Quinny with amusement. "I wasn't sure you were going to come through," Dukes said, playing to the group. He glanced around. "Remember this guy? This is Jimmy Quinn, the 'Nazi Killer.' I had him pay a visit to Jordan Rinaldi and his *putanna* wife. I hope he got the added bonus! Did you get a turn with the wife, Jimmy?"

Quinny smiled, hating this situation more by the second. Dukes was drunk. He wanted to throw the envelope at the guy and just leave, but he needed to play it cool if he was going to get paid. "Yeah, well . . . yeah," he said. "But all I could get was three Gs from Rinaldi . . ."

"That's more than I seen from that fuckin' pervert so far. Maybe your luck's changing." Dukes looked around the group. Took a hit from the whiskey tumbler in front of him and licked his upper lip. "This guy Quinn, he don't know how to catch a break. He's the only son of a bitch in history who almost lost a fixed fight."

The ancient gangsters all chuckled, and Quinny smiled and laughed along. "Which fight was that, Tony?"

"Listen to this guy. Which one you think? The Golden Gloves." He mugged for the other card players. "We all almost lost our asses that night. All you had to do was land one clean-looking punch and that Jamaican kid would have made it look like a realistic knockout. Instead, this shanty Irish prick gets dropped on his ass by the guy we paid to lose. You can't make this shit up. Thank Christ, he comes out with that crazy punch, like his old man laid on the Guv'nor—

remember that fucking circus? —and Rasta fazool finally got to take his scheduled nap."

The sound in the room seemed to be squelched out, the faces became blurry, Quinny felt like he needed to brace himself to keep from falling over. *I won that fucking fight. I won the Golden Gloves, just like I put down that fucking Nazi with one punch.* He felt himself starting to sweat, and he tried to think of his anger management tools, but he couldn't even remember where to start.

When he refocused on Dukes, the man was looking at him with concern, maybe regret, in his eyes. "I was just busting your balls, Jimmy. Don't tell me you thought that fight was square all these years . . ."

The other old men chuckled. Quinny glanced over at the young giant, who had stood up next to his card table.

"That fight was legit," Quinny said, barely controlling his voice. "I was in the ring, actually fighting, unlike you old fucks. Tyrus Raymond was trying to put me away, and I put him away."

Dukes raised a hand to the young giant, who had taken a step toward Quinny, and looked Quinny in the eye. "Just like your old man. Too dumb to know when you got it good. Let's have that envelope, Jimmy, and then maybe I'll let you just walk out of here, maybe I'll forgive and forget. You can come back and say sorry when you've had time to think."

Quinny took the envelope from his back pocket and held it up. He looked Dukes in the eye. "Tell you what, you fucking bootleg John Gotti: I'm gonna consider this the first payment for the forty grand you owe my dad. You only got thirty-seven grand to pay off now, or you can just give him the keys to the scrapyard, and we'll call it even."

All the old men stared, mouths open. Dukes looked at the young giant, almost sadly, and nodded.

Quinny didn't clock the Big Guy approaching him. He just at stared Dukes until he sensed the range was right, then he spun and leapt, lobbed a Superman punch into the center of the giant's chest. He'd show these motherfuckers what was real and what wasn't. Big Guy was knocked backward and threw a haphazard counterpunch like a man who'd never thrown a punch in his life. Quinny avoided the giant fist easily and started hooking off on the man's liver with his left, then rammed a right into the sternum. The guy had a lost, fearful look in his eye now. Quinny drew back to put him to sleep when Dukes caught hold of his arm.

All the wise guys stood. Dukes was trying to show that he still had it.

Quinny grinned, spun, and fired a one-two into Dukes's determined face, breaking teeth, causing blood to start dripping. He wanted the room to look like a bomb had gone off. Fuck Dukes and his endless stream of bullshit. And Quinny knew he'd get away with it too. A small part of his mind told him that Greaser Jack would take his side. He'd apologize on his way out, and it would be a story told for years to come . . . he just needed to *make* it out.

Then his brain exploded, and everything shut down for a moment.

Big Guy didn't know how to fight, but you didn't have to if you could get off a clean punch with three hundred pounds behind it. Quinny knew later that the man had taken aim and nailed him in the back of the head while he was distracted by Dukes.

As he tried get his bearings, he felt things other than fists slamming into him. The old men had swarmed, someone had a bat, someone had the cast iron skillet off the hotplate where they fried sausages, someone had a wooden plaque ripped off the wall. He tried to block, and to land punches, but they were coming from all angles.

Then it went black like an electrical cable had been snipped.

Quinny never knew what caused it, but for the first time in his life, he was stone-cold KO'd.

***

When he regained consciousness, his arms were outstretched on the card table with a bunch of wise guys holding him down by his forearms and wrists, a couple more sitting on his legs. He tasted blood in his mouth, and there was blood leaking down over one eye, causing him to blink and shake his head. Dukes was standing in front of him, blood smeared across his saggy face, strands of gray hair standing up crazily.

In his left hand, Dukes clutched two screwdrivers. a matching set, one flathead, one Phillips. In his right hand, he had an old, wooden-handled hammer.

Quinny immediately understood. He gave a great heave, almost got his right arm loose, but Big Guy—bloody-faced, sweating like a pig—refastened his hold on Quinny's wrist. The guy's grip was like a vise.

Quinny thought quickly, filled his lungs, and yelled, "JACK! Goddammit! Jack!" hoping the old mobster hadn't left the record store yet.

He looked back at Dukes, seeing if this ploy had any effect, but Dukes was eying the doorway, and Quinny glanced over.

Greaser Jack stood there, looking on.

"Jack!" Quinny said. "You gotta . . ."

But Jack's focus was on Dukes. He said, "Just the left, Tony. I still got a use for the right." Jack turned around and exited, pulling the door shut behind him.

Quinny couldn't see his left hand, but he felt Dukes put the point of the screwdriver to it, and he sensed the shift in weight as the hammer was raised. He might have said "*No* . . ." resignedly as the hammerhead thudded into the screwdriver handle.

And then he blacked out.

CHAPTER FIFTEEN: US VS. THEM

Quinny's cell phone rang. It was in his left front pocket. His hand was too bulky and sore to reach in. He had to reach across his body and use his right hand to retrieve the phone. It took him six or seven rings to finally slide it out, hit accept, and take the call.

"Greaser Jack wants a meeting," Bartley said. "Ten o'clock at Kings Plaza Diner. Be there."

"What?" he said. "No. Fuck that guy. He let them take my hand. I'm not meeting him anywhere."

"You either meet him at the diner or he'll come find you. You don't want that."

"Let him come," he said. "It won't be my first body and it probably won't be my last."

"Listen to me," his father said, "you're going to the diner at ten o'clock. He regrets what happened and he's gonna make it up to you."

"Really? He's gonna fill the fucking hole in my hand back in?" he said. "What if I see the fucker and stick a fork in his eye for what he did to me? He deserves worse."

"That would be unwise," Bartley said. "Go and hear him out. That's all there is to it. If Jack wanted you gone, we wouldn't be having this conversation. These guys aren't what they once were, but their balls haven't been cut off."

"Ten o'clock. Be there." Bartley hung up.

The diner was an hour away on foot, but Quinny felt like walking. His hate for Jack and his mafia buddies burned as hot as the wound through his palm. The mob were like half-assed celebrities where he grew up. Every person in the tri-state area with a vowel in their surname had a vague mob story. Their cousin's friend's uncle was Sammy the Bull. Vinny the Chin's brother, the priest, baptized their niece. They had a drink with Geno Durante at the Gemini Lounge where the DeMeo crew and the Westies chopped the bodies up. It made him cringe how much people gassed them up like they weren't just regular scumbags.

He met Jack for breakfast at the Kings Plaza Diner because there weren't any Jewish delis left since Seniors and Jay & Lloyd's went out of business, and Jack—not Jewish—only ate at Jewish delis. It was one of the busiest restaurants in Marine Park, but no matter how crowded, there was always a booth in back reserved for Jack.

Quinny gave a knowing nod to the pretty hostess with the dark curly hair and made his way to Jack's table. Every eyeball in the joint from the counters to the booths snuck a glance in his direction, some more slyly than others. The clientele was mostly retired cops, firefighters, teachers, nurses, bus drivers. If they bothered to look up from their fries, it meant Jack was already at his table—no doubt with his back to the wall, clocking whoever was coming his way. They were taking mental notes, trying to figure out why Quinny was there and what his involvement with the mob was. That's potentially useful information when he makes his boxing debut. Quinny and Jack's presence gave bored people a thrill.

Jack stood to give him a quick hug and pat on the back, hoping to avoid the awkwardness of a handshake, but Quinny was having none of it. He took a step back and extended his left hand. Jack looked at the mangled mitt with disgust.

The whole room was captivated by the tense standoff. The only sounds came from the kitchen—the head cook barking orders in Spanish, meat sizzling, pots clanging.

A nervous waitress appeared. Jack took a seat first. He ordered ham and eggs—no toast, no potatoes. Quinny took a deep breath before he sat across from Jack. He ordered a cheeseburger and disco fries.

"Years ago, I got the idea to take my meetings in old-fashioned kosher delis," Jack said. He was feeling nostalgic. "The feds weren't looking for me in places like that. They weren't set up with surveillance, so they got nothing but photos of me eating matzoh ball soup with a friend. Time moved on, the old deli owners retired, their kids didn't want to take over the business. Too busy looking at people doing goofy dances on their phones to run a restaurant."

Quinny stared at the old man. "So what?"

"You've been away. Maybe the whole world looks different to you," he said. "The only constant in Brooklyn is change. The names and faces come and go. Different groups still arrive in waves, and they bring all their bullshit with them. You know bars show college football on Saturday afternoons now. Hipsters brought that from the Midwest. Bros. Whatever they are. Besides bookies and degenerate gamblers, nobody in this borough gave a two-penny fuck about college football until the Wonder Breads took over North Brooklyn. You see, these dimwits went to football colleges, so they get all dicked up when Ohio State plays Michigan. So, we adapted. Their money's green, too. In ten years, there won't be a decent red sauce joint in Brooklyn, and you'll have to cross the Verrazano to Staten Island for scungilli. Fiorentino's is gone. New Corner is gone. Bubble tea and vegan dim sum are the present and future. Manicotti and gefilte fish are the past."

The waitress silently placed their orders in front of them and slinked away without refilling their water.

"Thanks for the history lesson, Jack," Quinny said. "Why the hell do you care who runs the Jewish deli? What the fuck is bubble tea? You know what, I don't give a shit." He slammed his forearms on the table, which made the silverware rattle. "What do you want from me? Haven't you done enough already?"

"My offer still stands—a hundred thousand in your pocket to fight that commie Roman Kashan. We bury this other thing with Tony Dukes. I put him out to pasture for you. He's out. We're square. Fight's still on if you want it."

Quinny's face went red. He felt his body heat up and his head felt like it was filled with static. It took everything he had not to lunge across the table and choke the old bastard.

"How am I supposed to beat this guy when I can't even make two fists?"

Jack shot him an impatient look. "How the fuck should I know? Show up, take a beating, and get paid. See if I care. Or just bang him out with your right hand. The guy's a tomato can. Hit him with that Bullhammer punch you won the Golden Gloves with, and he'll go to sleep."

"As long as Tony Dukes lives and breathes, this thing ain't over," Quinny said. "He ripped my father off for forty thousand bucks, and instead of making it right, he took action against me. Action that you sanctioned, by the way, but that's neither here nor there. I can't let it happen."

"You can't let that happen?" Jack said. He laughed. "Who the fuck are you to decide what happens?"

"I'm consequences!" he said. "Your guy's a dead man. He just doesn't know it yet. He thinks he's gonna get away with stealing from my family and butchering my hand. Like I said, I can't let it happen."

"Keep it copacetic, Quinny. This whole conversation is a courtesy to Tommy. For all I care, you and your bum father can freeze to death on the street. I liked you. I liked your old man. I tried, but you people just don't understand the way things work. A guy like you can't do shit to a guy like Dukes."

"What's stopping me, Jack? You?" Quinny said. "You might not know this, but It's not 1958 anymore. I could snap your feeble neck like a breadstick, right here, right now. I only need one good hand to do it. I could wrap my arm around your neck and pull your fucking head off your shoulders and there isn't a thing you can do about it. It's not like the old days when you had muscle around you. You're vulnerable, old man. You're alone now. You're alone when you go home to your wife. The only reason nobody takes a shot at you is because nobody wants your job anymore. Feds go after the boss, everybody knows that. The job's not attracting the best and brightest these days. Nobody wants to be the last dinosaur before extinction. Your whole thing only works when people are scared of you. I'm not scared of you, Greaseball Jack."

Jack turned up his lip, draped his damp napkin over his plate of untouched food, and shrugged his shoulders. He looked back down at his plate and smoothed out the napkin, covering the entire plate, and waved Quinny off.

Meeting over.

CHAPTER SIXTEEN: FUCK THE SCENE

Quinny walked a mile and a half from the Marine Park Inn to the B train on Kings Highway and East Sixteenth Street. He found a seat and rode the train for an hour and ten minutes before arriving at Broadway and Houston. The subway was still awful and overcrowded, but it wasn't nearly as dangerous as it was in the Koch, Dinkins, and Giuliani years when chaos and violence permeated every subway car. Normal people doing normal things outnumbered the crazies about fifty to one. *Back in the day, it was up close and personal—closer to a one-to-one ratio.*

He walked east on Houston and dipped into Bereket for some Turkish food. Quinny ordered a large lentil soup for lunch. Ender, the counter guy, remembered him. Here, the unofficial store policy was this: If you could beat Ender at arm wrestling, you got a free doner kebab. Quinny never came close to a free kebab. Ender was a beast twenty years ago and even more of a beast now. Nonetheless, his soup was on the house.

"Welcome home, champ," Ender said.

Quinny cupped his hands together, raised the bowl, said *fuck it* and didn't care if he looked like a maniac slurping his soup like an overgrown child. Somehow, it was even better than he remembered. He closed his eyes and focused on flavors so rare to his palate—cumin, fresh lemon, and smoked Urfa pepper.

After lunch, he hoofed it to the corner where the Bank nightclub used to be and hung a left, walking seven blocks before entering Tompkins Square Park. He paused at the open metal gate and took a giant gulp of air. Looking around, Quinny realized he hadn't been in a crowd this size since his first day in special housing.

The anxiety he felt was soon overtaken by disenchantment. A couple of hundred aging punk rockers crammed into the park, in too-tight band tees that displayed their beer bellies and muffin tops. The scene "kids" that came out for today's hardcore punk show were undeniably middle-aged. The annual Rebirth of Hardcore Pride festival was dedicated to reuniting the bands that created the soundtrack to their youth. It was clear to see that time had not been on anyone's side here but admitting that wasn't an option. The spirit of '94 stunk up the whole park.

Skinhead Carlos approached him head-on, wrapping his arms tightly around his old friend. He grunted and lifted him off the ground for a split second.

"Hey!" Quinny laughed.

"Damn, Quinny, it's good to see you out here," Carlos said.

"Glad to be here," Quinny said. "Been missing you for twenty years, bro."

Carlos didn't know what to say. He remained quiet. There was an awkward silence between them.

"Why do you look like Slater from *Saved by the Bell*? What's with the hair?" Quinny said.

"Can't be shaved for battle forever," Carlos said. "I hung up the boots and braces, and grew my hair in '94 after—"

"—You miss it?"

"Nah. It was just a haircut, bro. It was time to move on to the next thing, you know?"

"That's not what I mean," Quinny said. "Do you miss being Skinhead Carlos? Do you miss rolling with the Graveyard Stompers? Cracking skulls and shit?"

"I'm supposed to say I don't," Carlos said, his face breaking into a grin, "but you know I do, motherfucker."

Carlos reached into the pockets of his cargo shorts and pulled out two metal combination locks and a white gym sock. "You never know, right?" he said. He shoved the locks into the sock and gave it a twirl.

"If it kicks off, I know you got my back," Quinny said. "I can't exactly use both hands."

"Yeah . . ." Carlos said. "Heard about that. It was fucked up what they did."

"Sure was. It would be a shame if Tony Dukes caught a lock to the skull."

Before he could answer, Tommy came up behind them and wrapped his arms around Carlos and Quinny. Quinny barely noticed Tommy slink off, though, because there she was.

Justine stood at a distance.

"Damn, Jus," Carlos said as he eyed her up and down, "that filmmaker life has been good to you."

The new Justine didn't punch him in the nose and tell him to fuck off. She accepted the so-called compliment with a fake smile, touching the palm of her hand to his chest. "Thanks," she said, moving in for a hug. She slid her hands from his back to his biceps and gave them a squeeze, then abruptly went back to looking at her phone.

It stung for Quinny to watch her touching Carlos like that. He still felt like a teenager in love, and like an asshole for feeling that way about a girl who clearly didn't give a shit.

Tommy power walked through the grass toward Quinny with a beer in his hand. He wore a short-sleeve gingham button-front shirt and black slacks. The slacks were dorky and made him seem older than his thirty-four years. Quinny knew he was some king shit finance guy who managed a private equity fund with mob money. It was the worst kept secret in New York.

Thing is, Tommy also did federal time. He ran a boiler room for Greaser Jack out of college and became a top earner for the Fortunato family bringing in just under what the made guys did on sports betting and heroin. Tommy eventually got jammed up with price manipulation and securities fraud, but he only did a cup-of-coffee sentence in Club Fed.

"My man," Tommy said. He handed Quinny a beer.

Quinny took a long swig out of the glass bottle. "Jesus, fuck, what kind of beer is that? It tastes like a dog's asshole."

"It's an IPA from our brewery," Tommy said dryly. "I forgot; you missed the entire craft beer revolution."

"I didn't miss shit," he said.

Justine turned back to face the group, still half-engrossed in a text conversation.

"Did *I* miss anything?" she asked.

"Yeah. I'm about to invite Carlos to Tony Dukes's boot party," Quinny said. "Seems like he's down. Maybe you can film us bashing the guy, release it as a documentary. I'll go to prison for a couple of decades, and you'll be in France winning awards and yelling, 'Free Jimmy Quinn.' But you'll never pick up the phone. You got time, but you ain't got time for me, girl."

Justine went stone-faced.

"Forget about Tony Dukes," Tommy said. "He's not worth the energy."

"It might be fun to kick his teeth out," Carlos said, "for old times' sake."

"Burn his house down. Fuck that guy," Justine said.

"Is it more cinematic that way?" Quinny asked.

"More dramatic," she said. "More *effective.*"

"It would be my honor to serve twenty years to deliver you another award-winning film,

Queen Justine." Quinny bowed down like a loyal servant.

"Fuck you, Quinny," she said. "All I did was give you what you wanted."

"No," he said. "You gave me everything but that."

"It's called a narrative," she said. "It's not my fault you didn't know what to do with it."

"Damn," Tommy said. "Why do you guys have to come out the gate being awkward?"

"Don't try to smooth things over, Tommy. This is bullshit and I'm gonna speak on it. It's part of my narrative," Quinny said.

They all laughed. Justine laughed the hardest.

"It's good you're all laughing, because this whole thing is a joke, but I'm not laughing. I'm looking at a celebration of youth culture for the middle aged, and it's fucking nauseating."

Quinny noticed Justine filming with her phone but kept talking.

"What the fuck is hardcore about any of this?" he said. "Reardon's a yuppie finance guy, Carlos is a suburban dad, and Justine went full Hollywood. You're the three least punk rock people in the world."

It was still daylight in the park when the DJ stopped playing aggressive music and put on a recording of the Om mantra on a loop. The decidedly un-mystical-looking crowd let out an excited cheer and pressed forward.

The Middle Path, a recently reunited straight edge and Buddhist band from the early

’90s, took the stage. Truth is, they weren’t particularly popular back then, but subculture folks don’t often remember things the way they actually were.

People were filing into the park from all directions. The crowd swelled until there were thousands of people to see a band who could barely draw a crowd of a hundred in their heyday.

The guitarist played the intro riff to “Killing Mara.” It electrified the crowd. A full-on circle pit opened up in the middle of the park.

The drums crashed. The singer ran across the stage and did one of the choreographed flying punches that adorned their T-shirts at the merch booth. After singing a lyric, he pointed the mic to the people in the front and, karaoke-style, they sang his words back to him.

For that moment, the crowd had no unaffordable mortgage payment, no dead-end job they hated, no kids they never wanted, no boring spouse who didn’t understand them. They were wild and free. Until the set ended. Then, the adrenaline wore off and the nostalgia ran thin. They were left with their present-day selves again.

“This is not hardcore,” Quinny said directly into Justine’s phone before slapping it out of her hand.

Hc turned his back and pulled an Irish exit before the headliners even went on.

He had an excuse for why his life didn’t move on from that of an eighteen-year-old hardcore kid, but this crowd, they had options, they chose to stay frozen in time. Quinny spent his years inside reliving and glamorizing his hardcore past. Now that past and present merged, he felt embarrassed. He wanted nothing to do with it. *Leave it to the young.* Quinny kept walking until he descended the stairs of the subway station, disappearing into the darkness.

He heard panting and saw Tommy run up to him. “Quinny, you fuck,” Tommy said. “I can’t believe you made me chase after you.”

“Look, Tommy, I was just upset with Justine. I didn’t mean to take it out on you.”

“But you’re a thousand percent right. I just want you to know that. I’ll never stop appreciating you for everything you did when we were kids. You saved my fucking life, Quinny. I got your training camp all set up down in Florida. It’s all about looking forward, not looking back for you. It’s the least I could do.”

“You don’t gotta tell me, Tommy. You’re the only real motherfucker. You never forgot. You didn’t let me rot in there. You’re the only friend I ever had. Everybody else was an acquaintance or a user. Go back to the show. Have fun with your friends.”

CHAPTER SEVENTEEN: BLOOD ON MY HANDS

Quinny flew down to Miami in basic economy with Tommy and his father. He'd never been on a plane before, so he didn't know the difference. It seemed fine to him but everyone else in his section complained. Bartley, a man who'd flown only once before—when he emigrated to the US—acted put out like he was an international playboy who only traveled by Learjet.

"It used to be nicer," he said. Everything, according to him: the food, the seats, the service, used to be better. Even the flight attendants used to be better looking. "They stopped being hot when they stopped being stewardesses," he said. But they weren't better looking then—that's a lie people like Bartley tell themselves. No different than the middle-aged nostalgia chasers in the park cosplaying as the sixteen-year-old hardcore kids they used to be.

Things have always been shit and garbage. They were shitty then, and they're still shitty. Basic economy was just fine. To Quinny, who spent the majority of the past thirteen years in solitary confinement, a cramped seat with its embedded TV screen was more than enough. His father was downright insulted that the airline charged them for the bags they brought onboard.

Tommy joked that they charged extra for you to take a piss, so Quinny held it in for five hours.

The guy next to him sat half in his lap the whole flight, lounging comfortably like King Farouk. Whenever His Highness looked like he was about to doze off, Quinny tapped his knee into the seat to jostle him awake. *Fuck him. If you make me miserable, I'll make you miserable too.*

The woman seated on his other side was another prize. She ate what looked like leftover chicken out of a Tupperware with her hands, then had the nerve to remove her shoes and stink the joint up. Since Quinny was eating clean, he was prepared. He countered her offensive snack with his own—bananas and hard-boiled eggs from his gym bag. By the time he was finished, her shoes were back on, and she was breathing into the sleeve of her sweater. *Mission accomplished.*

One thing Quinny did know is that Greaser Jack would have put his team in first class. Despite all his Wall Street money, Tommy was a pragmatist at heart. Perpetually single, he slept in a twin bed. He only wore merino wool T-shirts because they repelled odor-causing bacteria "They only have to be washed every ten wears," he claimed.

He made them take a free shuttle bus to the hotel.

Tommy was even stingy on somebody else's dime. Even though the Loews, a fancy hotel in South Beach, offered him three rooms on the arm, he told them that one would be more than enough. Tommy and both Quinns shared a single room like college kids on spring break.

Bartley insisted that Quinny sleep on the floor. "Soft beds make soft fighters," he said. "Who wants to wake up at four a.m. to run six miles when you're sleeping on silk sheets?" *Ugh. This again.*

If he was really serious about the fight, his father said, he'd sleep on a bench in the park. Jack Dempsey slept in Central Park before becoming the number one contender for the heavyweight title. When training for a fight, Big Joe Joyce dipped his hands in petrol and slept rough. Bartley Quinn himself slept in Marine Park and only ate bologna sandwiches before putting the Guv'nor to sleep. The old-timers thought it hardened the spirit, but Quinny's spirits were already granite. The hole through the palm of his hand took care of that.

His hand was still fucked. He could almost make a fist but couldn't squeeze it tightly due to the pain and swelling. He found out this version of "bareknuckle" didn't mean bare fists. Fighters were allowed to wrap their hands, as long as their knuckles were exposed. He could conceal his injury under wraps, literally. Since it was taking place on a reservation, there wouldn't be an athletic commission to perform prefight medicals. If he showed up with a pulse, he'd be good to go.

Collect the check, kick half up to Jack, then give ten thousand to his dad and ten thousand to Tommy for the training camp. He'd have more than enough left over to buy his dad out of his mess. *Get Dad his shop back. Get myself an apartment and a car. Live like a human being for once.*

Training camp was a nightmare. Quinny couldn't throw punches or block like a gloved boxer without causing further damage to his injured hand, and his team wanted him to save whatever he had for the fight. So, he didn't hit anything. They had Quinny on a fitness regimen of early morning runs and a sadistic sparring program where all he did was defend. The idea was to make Kashan tire himself out by missing Quinny and then drop the Bullhammer on him.

He worked out of a Latin gym in Little Havana. The fighters there were pros—seasoned Cuban defectors, Venezuelan cabbies with a boxing side hustle, and up-and-coming Puerto Rican kids. Quinny played human punching bag for all of them. "Sparring" here meant trying to slip or block punches by catching them on his forearms. No matter. Quinny was there to perfect his defense, not look good sparring. They all took turns beating the shit out of him. Even though he had a hundred pounds on some of those guys. He couldn't hit back so he took the L every time.

Even as an eighteen-year-old, Quinny was useless at slipping. Twenty years later, his reflexes were shot to shit. He was slow and sluggish. He could barely get out of his own way, let alone out of the way of incoming punches.

Bartley's solution was covering his face with the forearms in a high guard. Quinny kept them moving by pantomiming running his broken hands through his hair—an old school bareknuckle defensive tactic called the Crazy Monkey. It was effective and saved some brain cells. There was one problem: You can't block a punch and return fire with your hands on top of your head. You either blocked or you punched. Using the Crazy Monkey for offense was a fool's mission, but he didn't have much of a choice on account of not being able to throw a punch with his left hand. He was going to block until it was time to drop the right-hand bomb.

Once he got comfortable with the Crazy Monkey and blocked all incoming punches, he'd take a step back and fake a Bullhammer at his sparring partner to get the timing right. There was a method to Bartley's madness. *This shit is going to work like a charm.*

Team Quinn watched video of the guy he was going to fight. Roman Kashan. A former heavyweight champion in mixed martial arts, he was a frightening specimen in his prime. Big punching power, but sloppy technique. He loaded up on his punches, overcommitted, and dropped his hands when he threw for power. That left his chin out on a silver platter for a counterpunch. Quinny envisioned clipping this guy with the Bullhammer so many times, it was like it had already happened.

Unfortunately, Kashan threw wide Russian hooks. They looked sloppy, but they were the product of a high-level Soviet-era technique that takes years to perfect. None of the fighters at the gym could mimic them in sparring, so Bartley stepped in and faked it. Wide, casting hooks are deceptively quick looping punches that take a while to get used to. Quinny let his father pound on him in the gym. Soon he was comfortable in the pocket with John Wayne punches whizzing by his head. *Get out your frustrations with life and everyone in it, Pop.*

On the street, fans thought Kashan's chin was iffy, but what they didn't know was Jimmy Quinn's left hand was iffier. The odds should have leaned heavily toward the Russian, due to his level of competition and recent activity, but the bettors thought his chin was cracked and it was a pick 'em fight. Kashan got KO'd in his last three MMA fights. You can't unscramble eggs. This was a classic matchup between a has-been and a never-was. But the never-was happened to be a prison champion who'd killed a man with his bare hands, and there's a certain cachet to that. Some bettors saw it as a chinless wonder against a man with a legit kill-shot punch.

Miami was a ridiculous place. The smartest people went to New York, the most attractive people flocked to Los Angeles, and the biggest cheeseballs were inexplicably drawn to Miami. *What a sewer.* To Quinny, Ocean Drive looked like a bunch of day-shift strippers palling around with the cast of the *Jersey Shore.* Every restaurant and storefront blasted a hip-hop song about asses in English or *culos* in Spanish.

He spent his time in South Pointe Park near the southern tip of Miami Beach. He did sprints and squats and ab work and rounds of shadow boxing outside to get the Bullhammer timing down.

A kid with a fresh fade, maybe seven or eight years old, walked over to Quinny.

“We got bitches. White bitches, Chinese bitches, Black bitches,” he said. He handed Quinny a business card printed with an address and the initials DT. Pimps threw this child a couple of bucks when somebody used his card to buy ass. Quinny felt bad for the little dude, but he was in no position to help him out. He was stone-cold broke and with the most important event of his life coming up, he didn’t need a beef with the cops or whatever pimp this kid was working for. He chased the kid away, but the little guy came back again the next day. He leaned against a palm tree and watched Quinny work out, then mimicked his shadow boxing at a distance. Little man could mime the Bullhammer pretty well. Quinny got a kick out of it. For a second, he had the urge to run over and adjust the kid’s form. He could have taught him a thing or two. But, nah. It was too late. *By the time you’re seven, you already are who you’re going to be.* The kid was headed to an early grave or a long life in a cage.

Due to a complete lack of walking around money, Quinny stayed sober. Brooklyn people don’t use “party” as a verb, but down there, everybody did. Instead of going to tacky Collins Avenue, he stayed in the park or walked along the beach until it was time for dinner. Tommy arranged a meal delivery service to bring everyone breakfast and dinner. It was all veggies and smoothies, but as Bartley was fond of saying, "If it's free, it's for me." Quinny sure as hell wasn't going to turn it down.

***

The air conditioning in the halls of the hotel hit Quinny just right. It was the most powerful AC he'd ever felt. And the carpeting in the hallway was so soft, it had the same bounce as a boxing ring. Quinny felt content, like everything was going according to plan.

He pulled the key card out of the pocket of his basketball shorts, held it to the reader on the door until the light turned green, and turned the handle. Next thing he knew, he felt something crash into the back of his head. He fell forward on his hands and knees and puked up some blood.

Quinny was woozy and the back of his head felt hot. He tried to piece together what happened. A man's voice screamed, "You think you can cut me out, you prick?!" followed by two loud puffs of air. Later, he understood them as gunshots muffled by a silencer.

Tony Dukes had put two rounds behind Tommy's right ear as he typed on his laptop at the little desk in their hotel room. His slack body slid down the chair and onto the floor with a muted thud.

His friend bled out on the floor as Dukes continued yelling. Quinny felt like he had water in his ears and cotton in his brain. He couldn't make out most of what Dukes said. Something about being forced to retire. Dukes must have bashed Quinny over the head with the gun, then bum-rushed the door. A push-in job. It was a brazen move, taking out Greaser Jack's protégé Tommy Reardon like that. Dukes should have also taken out Quinny when he could. He had to have known what would come next. If Quinny was still breathing, Quinny was his consequences.

Suddenly, Bartley flew out of the bathroom and tackled Dukes, knocking the gun out of his hand. Pretty spry for a broken-down old junkman. The two of them rolled around on the ground, grunting, until Quinny snapped out of his stupor and got back on his feet. Kicking the gun into the far corner of the room, he loosened his arms like he was in the gym getting ready to spar. He bounced for a few seconds, staying light on his feet, and shadowboxed to warm up his shoulders.

"Jesus Fucking Christ, boyo," his father said between gasps. "A little help!"

He took a deep breath. Tony Dukes was his sparring partner now.

The elder Quinn rushed to Tommy Reardon. He crouched over his body, told him to wake up, and shook him vigorously by the shoulders. He got no answer. Antonio LoDuca cowered at the foot of the bed. He covered up like a scared animal hiding from a predator. The man accepted his fate. There was no fight left in him.

He should have been six feet under for ripping off Bartley and giving his son a crucifixion wound. Bartley didn't even try to restrain Quinny or talk him out of what he was about to do.

Quinny lunged and used his left hand to blast Dukes in the soft spots—his gut and his throat. Each strike to Dukes' body hurt Quinny's hand more than it hurt him. His punching power was completely gone from the southpaw side, as dead as Tommy. He still couldn't completely close his fist. It took him four clean left hooks to the liver to drop an old man. *Pathetic.*

Dukes crawled away, trying to get to his feet. Quinny kicked him in the head.

Dukes collapsed on his face.

Quinny turned him over and mounted him, landing punch after punch with his right hand until he couldn't feel his good hand anymore. His body bypassed the pain and just went straight to shock. He rained down hard elbows and forearms to preserve what was left of his hands. When he got tired from that, he used his forehead as a battering ram against the bridge of Dukes's nose.

Dukes's face was hamburger meat. His skull was caved in on one side. That finished the game.

Quinny rolled over, completely drained. His whole body shook but the anger and pain were gone. His mind went blank. Quinny threw up three times, then drifted off like Rip Van Winkle.

He woke up with a massive headache and his hands caked in blood. His stitches had burst open, and his hand leaked blood from a now-gaping wound. He shuffled into the bathroom and tried stuffing the hole in his hand with crumpled up toilet paper, but it was a losing battle.

There were still two dead bodies in a hotel room. Bartley sat on his bed, talking to a soft man in a tan linen suit. Probably a lawyer. Three Blackwater types, ex-military for sure, were swiftly cleaning up the mess. It was all very organized and dispassionate. Quinny hated himself for letting this happen to his closest friend—the closest thing he had to a brother. If he hadn't provoked Dukes for fucking over his dad, Tommy wouldn't be dead.

Quinny caused this. He felt too guilty to be heartbroken.

The lawyer walked over and squatted next to Quinny. "There's not going to be a problem with the law," he said, "but just in case, let me assure you that you're not going back to prison. Self-defense. Temporary insanity. It's Florida, for fuck's sake. We've got stand your ground. You're covered."

He stood and walked away before doubling back. "Give Jack Fortunato a call within the hour. Drink some water first and get your head together. He wants to hear this directly from you."

Quinny tried to process everything that happened, but it felt unreal. Not like a dream. Just like some shit that never really happened, except it totally happened. His first clear thought finally broke through the fog. *There's no way I'm gonna be able to fight Kashan with an open wound and a broken brain.*

Quinny wasn't big on emotional outbursts, but he was being overtaken by a new feeling. The pain he felt wasn't sharp like a right hook—it was the deep ache of knowing the only person who ever respected him and asked for nothing in return was gone. Quinny fucked that up like he fucked everything else up.

The world needs more men like Tommy Reardon. You were genuine, Tommy. That's the best thing that can be said about anyone.

He patted his slumped friend on the head. There wouldn't be a funeral. No one could know what happened in the hotel room. The dull pain in his heart swelled up into his throat and tears collected in the corners of his eyes. Quinny hadn't cried in thirty years, but now was as good a time as any.

CHAPTER EIGHTEEN: IT'S CLOBBERIN' TIME

Justine Obscene texted Quinny that she touched down in Miami and wanted to see him. She'd come to cover his bareknuckle fight with Roman Kashan, which she called "Nazi Killer vs. Russian Mob Dracula."

She thought she was being cute, but they both knew this fight was unfairly stacked. He was supposed to be the victim and Justine was gonna be lady Weegee—the celebrated crime scene photographer there to capture the blood and gore on film. After what happened to Tommy, he should have been immune to her charms, but that text predictably reignited something in him. She complained to Quinny that visiting Miami was about as pleasurable as last month's parasitic pinworm infection, which she picked up squatting in a warehouse with climate activists. She told him she'd had abortions that were more fun than the bars lining Collins Avenue in South Beach. Quinny was somehow charmed. He agreed to meet her and film scenes for the *Graveyard Stomper* documentary.

Pull it together. Justine might be useful right now. Justine could score heroin. She's good at shit like that. The black stuff would dull the physical, and emotional, pain. Vicodin was bullshit. It just made Quinny constipated on top of the hurt.

Quinny arrived at the pool at The Standard on Biscayne Bay a half hour late for their interview. Justine was shooting B-roll. She seemed entertained by the orange tans, gummy bear breast implants, and Brazilian butt lifts. It was a cosmetic dermatologist's wonderland of overfilled faces, micro bladed eyebrows, lipo-sculpted abs, calf implants, steroids, human growth hormone, clenbuterol, cocaine, and elaborate hair systems. Documentaries love a freakshow, and these people who bleach their assholes, get knee lifts, and inject their stomach fat into their cocks were certified freaks.

Justine filmed Quinny clocking a tan plastic surgery monstrosity with a cat face and a huge ass as she looked back at him on her jiggle-walk to the pool.

"That's gross," he said, "but, I would totally fuck her. What can I say, I'm a man. And nobody can tell what I'm thinking with these Ace Rothstein glasses."

"Everyone can tell," she said.

Quinny wasn't the only man in South Florida wearing oversized Blu Blocker sunglasses, just the only one under seventy. He wore them to conceal his red eyes—raw from crying over Tommy. He hadn't slept yet and spent the night aimlessly walking the streets and chewing handfuls of synthetic morphine.

He didn't carry himself with his usual swagger. His hands were both wrapped in gauze, and his body language was sunken and contracted. He was retreating into himself, like a man who was too distracted to win a fight. Or like a man who might not make it through the night.

He felt even worse. He was pumped with hydromorphone to dull the pain, but it dulled his senses. He'd finished three-quarters of the bottle in the first two days. It was meant to last two weeks. Groaning as he sat across from Justine under a pool umbrella, he took the ridiculous glasses off.

She either didn't notice his red-rimmed eyes or didn't care to ask.

"Where's your dad? I miss that old grouch," she said.

Quinny took a second to let his eyes focus in the shade. His brain was firing slower than usual.

"Dad's going to be passed out drunk for the foreseeable future." Quinny chuckled at the absurdity of his situation. "You know, as a kid, I thought both of my parents were epileptic because of all the times they fell down and stayed down on the floor."

"Oh yeah?" she said, absent-mindedly. "Pretty sure you never mentioned that."

"I didn't," he said. "I wouldn't. It's not like you'd feel sorry for me. It's not like my life went to the dogs. Not like yours, right?"

"Right," she said tentatively. Justine wasn't sure where he was going with this.

"Exactly," he grumbled. His eyes were closed. "I didn't experience those dog days in Russia like you and your brother Vadim. Hey, are you gonna interview Kashan in your native language?"

Quinny watched her squirm a little and struggle to maintain composure. It was clear she didn't expect him to remember her lie from the '90s. Justine wasn't accustomed to being called on her bullshit.

He opened his eyes and looked into hers. "It's not like *everything* you've ever told me was a lie, right?"

She remained silent.

"What are you here for?" he slurred. "Wasn't it enough to ruin my life once? You had to come back for more?"

"I'm here for your fight tomorrow," she said. "People care about you enough for me to shoot a follow-up movie. But don't get it twisted—they only give a shit because of my documentary. I made you famous, not the other way around. Why else do you think they'd pay you six figures to fight this brain-damaged Belarusian?"

"I think he's going to kill me," Quinny said, "not just beat me. Zero hype. I'm not sure I'm gonna leave that ring with my life. You know how the guys who train pit bulls for dogfights sometimes feed them an old, wounded shelter dog? I'm the mutt from the pound—he's gonna eat me alive."

"You've got to believe in yourself. Mindset is what separates the best from the re—"

"Justine! I can't throw a punch with one of my hands. I'm doped up on opioids to numb the pain. I'm puking from a concussion. I can't sleep. My only real friend died right in front of me, and I let some mob goons dispose of his body in the

Everglades like he was never here. My dad's a drunk. I have no one in my corner. No one's looking out for me. You're talking to a dead man, Justine."

"With the odds stacked against him, the noble Nazi Killer persisted," she said. "Americans love a second chance story—a redemption narrative. They love the underdog pulling off the improbable victory and finally living up to his potential. This is your hero's journey, Quinny."

Quinny stood up. "Look, I only agreed to meet you because I thought you'd either try to fuck me to get your story or you could get me heroin. I know we're not gonna bang, but I'm running out of Oxys and morphine pills, and to tell you the truth, they ain't cutting it. Tommy said you were making a movie about sex offenders who live in a tent city because they aren't allowed to live near schools or parks. Those creeps probably bang a lot of H. Could you hook it up?"

Justine nodded yes.

Quinny stood and lumbered off to drain the minibar in his hotel room and catch a nap.

The fight was supposed to be on an indigenous reservation. The fight was well-promoted—the flyers said ex-MMA champion Roman "The Butcher" Kashan vs. undefeated jailhouse boxing champion Jimmy "Nazi Killer" Quinn. Everyone and their bookie was talking about the convicted murderer who killed a white supremacist with a punch. In fact, the original venue had to be moved to a bigger one to squeeze in all the fans hungry for the fight. The match was being shown live on a cable network called Combat TV. It was all tied up in a neat little noose. Bribes were paid, the new venue was secured, the rights were sold, and the athletic commission was going to allow Quinny to fight no matter what condition he was in.

The crowd that gathered at Banco Sol Arena the next night was awful, even by boxing standards. They came to witness ultraviolence, not a sporting competition. The undercard was an atrocity. Whoever booked the thing made the matches too even—every single fight went to a decision. The women's title fight, a bloodbath, went the distance and looked like Carrie left prom to fight Countess Bathory.

Most of the crowd was learning for the first time that boxing gloves actually allow fighters to throw more powerful punches—the kind that end fights—without breaking their hands. Bare fists do not equal harder punches, but they do burst skin like a balloon and make a bloody mess. After three bloodstained ordeals in a row, the crowd started to feel a little uneasy about being there.

The music stopped and the arena went completely dark. The crowd's collective anxiety turned to excitement. They jumped to their feet and cheered him on. Jimmy Quinn made his ring walk with a cut man appointed by the state athletic commission by his side as Inside Out's "No Spiritual Surrender" played over the PA. He was so doped up that he didn't try to look cool or intimidating at all. He smiled wide and visualized the hundred thousand dollars that was going to bail him and his father out of the hole they were in. The H he snorted in the dressing room gave him a warm, pleasant feeling.

He focused on the new life this fight would buy him, but he couldn't ignore the cheers he heard from the crowd when he entered the ring and raised his hands. A wave of optimism almost knocked him over.

The lights went down again. This time, the harsh sounds of Belarusian trap metal group Mora Prokaza came over the system. Roman Kashan entered the arena, flanked by his expressionless team in matching tracksuits. He flipped his long caveman hair to the side and flashed the camera his trademark red fang mouthpiece.

"Where is my gun? Where is my gun?" That was the only lyric Quinny could make out. This man was supposed to be frightening, but Quinny thought his goofy vampire schtick made him look like a cornball.

In bareknuckle fights, boxers don't start at opposite corners of the ring. The ring isn't even a ring. Bouts take place in a circle with a twenty-two-foot diameter and four thick ropes. Instead of beginning each round at a distance, they "toe the line" within three feet of each other before the bell rings. That means more action, faster.

Quinny had a vague sense that he was being led to his execution. Fortunately, he was too high to be afraid. He felt calm and even a little drowsy. If he wasn't surrounded by ten thousand bloodthirsty fight fans screaming for violence, he would have laid down and taken a nap.

During their face-off, it was clear that this matchup was a lot more lopsided than the other fights that night. Kashan was taller and had twenty-six pounds on Quinny, but it seemed like fifty pounds when he stood next to the guy. Quinny was lean and strong, but he looked like somebody's dad about to fight a professional wrestler.

The fight started when the referee screamed, "Knuckle up." Kashan threw a tornado of punches and Quinny fought out of the Crazy Monkey stance. Crouched down low with his hands on top of his head, he blocked all of Kashan's head punches with his forearms. When Kashan tried to punch him in the ribs, he blocked those shots with his elbows.

Quinny looked slick as fuck out there. A U-S-A chant broke out in the crowd. Kashan was befuddled by the defense Quinn's dad taught him. Quinny heard women in the crowd scream "I love you." For the first time in a very long time, he felt alive, he felt like a human being.

Kashan didn't land anything serious in the first two-minute round. Quinn didn't throw anything serious but caught Kashan's attention with a few well-placed right crosses, feeling his opponent out for the eventual Bullhammer. Miracle of miracles, Quinny survived the first round and dominated it.

When round two started, his luck held for a while, but between rounds Kashan's corner adapted and he settled into a new strategy—draping his left arm over Quinny's neck and punching him with his right hand. This is perfectly legal in bareknuckle boxing. Kashan used his size and strength to nullify Quinny's technical excellence.

Quinny was a bloody mess. He countered Kashan's tentacle grip by striking the Belarusian's face with his shoulder when he pulled in close. After the third shoulder strike, Kashan's nose was obviously broken, and his right eye was beginning to swell.

"Knock it off with the shoulder shit," the ref warned him. Apparently, hitting someone with a sharp shoulder is illegal in bareknuckle. Both fighters were wearing crimson masks of blood.

Quinny pawed at Kashan's eye and made the cut even bigger.

One round even. One round for Jimmy Quinn.

Kashan came out aggressive for round three. He was able to land combinations. Kashan broke through the Crazy Monkey defense by pushing Quinny's hands down so he couldn't block.

Kashan landed hard punches and Quinny got lit up like a Christmas tree. Quinny tried throwing punches back, but it was clear the reaction drills he did in training were no substitute for live offensive sparring. The timing of his punches was way off.

Quinny made the commitment to get aggressive and take some risks. He used his mangled hands as best he could, throwing hands like he was swinging a tomahawk. Trying to land with the bottom of his palm instead of the knuckles was his best bet. The move is called a hammer fist. They're legal in this outlaw sport, and they were fucking Kashan up. Quinny was winning the round on pure aggression.

In the final seconds, Quinny battered Kashan into the ropes. The Butcher was getting butchered. Quinny landed a dozen unanswered punches. Kashan looked as if he could no longer defend himself. Quinny knew it was time to finish him. He wound up and threw a full power hammer fist at a helpless Kashan, who immediately came to life, slipped Quinny's telegraphed punch, and landed an uppercut with his hands down at his waist. Quinny never saw it coming. The punches you don't see are the ones that hurt the worst.

Quinny got knocked down. His vision became fuzzy, but he could make out the referee standing over him and Kashan across the ring. He wanted to stay down and drift off. It was a familiar feeling, like a few days earlier when Tony Dukes pistol whipped him and killed Tommy. Quinny was hurt, but more than that, he was angry. He used his dead best friend as motivation and somehow made it to his feet at the count of nine. Quinny felt dazed and swayed like a Bowery bum. He tried to survive by blocking punches with the Crazy Monkey, but it wasn't working this time. Kashan was destroying his face. His vision was obscured by blood spilling into his eyes. His left cheekbone felt caved in. His forehead felt like it tripled in size.

Jimmy Quinn was saved by the bell.

After the bell, Kashan talked shit to Quinny who replied by instinctively headbutting the Belarusian on the nose during the break in action. The round was close, but it went to Roman Kashan because of the knockdown.

Quinny's face leaked like a faucet. The cut man he'd just met tried in vain to stop the bleeding. Then, the ref took a point away from Quinny for the illegal headbutt.

The zombie version of Quinny ambled out for the fourth round. The crowd roared. Underneath the "Quinny" chants he could hear people screaming, "stop the fight" and "throw in the towel." He was happy that he didn't have anyone who cared about him in his corner to throw in the towel and end this nightmare. On the other side of the ring, Kashan's corner tended to his cuts and offered advice in Russian.

Kashan went back to holding and hitting. Quinny saw it happening, but he couldn't move fast enough and didn't have the strength to do anything about it. Quinny felt as helpless and defenseless as when Tony Dukes and his soldiers drove a screwdriver through his palm.

The ref separated Kashan's vise grip from Quinny's shoulder and called for a break, probably saving whatever brain matter Quinny had left. As soon as he had a split second to react, Quinny headbutted Kashan again. Watching the wound expand at the top of

Kashan's nose instantly cheered Quinny up. Kashan looked like he'd taken a machete to the eyebrow and bled like a victim in a slasher film. The ref took another point away from Quinny. One more foul and he'd get disqualified.

Roman Kashan was up big on the judges' scorecards. At this point, the only chance Quinny had of winning was by knockout. Even his head and elbows couldn't take the Belarusian down. The ref should have stopped the fight. Quinny couldn't even hold his arms up to block anymore. He was completely unable to protect himself. Kashan looked like he was about to get the knockout when the bell rang to end the fourth round.

Quinny flopped on his ass in the middle of the ring. He couldn't even make it to his corner. The ref tried to pick him up and usher him to his corner, but Quinny was dead weight.

Bartley came out of nowhere, probably the bar area, and drunkenly staggered into the ring to help his son up. The father slurred in his son's ear, "You've been here before, son. You have a secret weapon that this fucker doesn't know about. This guy is fucked, and he doesn't even know it. He thinks he's winning. He thinks he's got you. He's about to get knocked the fuck out."

Bartley's appearance and words felt like a shot of adrenaline to Quinny. He spryly got back to his feet. Somehow, the ref allowed the fight to continue. He could have called it because of the beating Quinny was taking; he could have disqualified Quinny for refusing to go to his corner, or for Quinny and Bartley flagrantly violating the one-minute time limit between rounds. The ref was in somebody's pocket, and that somebody wanted a televised execution.

Bartley continued slurring instructions. "You know what to do. Just listen for my voice, I'll call for it. He won't know what hit him."

The final round began. It was the same shit, different round. But this time Quinny looked like he was trying to block punches with his face on purpose. He needed to lull Kashan into a false sense of security and overconfidence if he was going to make the Bullhammer work, and that's what he needed to get the knockout and win this fight.

Kashan fell for it and bombed away with looping, casting hooks, trying to end the fight.

He was getting sloppy and overconfident.

That's when Bartley screamed, "Drop the Bullhammer!"

Quinny did his best to recreate the magic of his improbable Golden Gloves win. He waited for Kashan to miss with a hook, then wound up, took a giant step forward, cocked his arm at a ninety-degree angle, used his hips to generate power, and whipped his arm like a mace. He committed fully to the Bullhammer and threw it with perfect technique. He anticipated the pain he was about to feel in his hand as it landed on Kashan's chin and thought about the spectacular knockout that would follow and how video clips would go viral.

Kashan pivoted forty-five degrees and the Bullhammer missed by a mile. Quinny's attempt to finish the fight looked comical and amateurish. He was off balance, slow, and overcommitted to a punch that had no chance of landing. Kashan clipped Quinny's chin with a clean left-hand counter and Quinny faceplanted with a disturbing quickness, like he was knocked out before he even hit the ground.

The referee waved it off. Fight over.

"The winner by way of knockout . . . and new Police Gazette Bareknuckle Boxing Heavyweight Champion of the world, Roman 'The Butcher' Kashan!" the ring announcer bellowed. The crowd was hushed, stunned by the brutality of the finish. They had violence in their minds, but this proved to be too much.

Quinny wasn't moving.

Flat on his back with his arms and legs loosely splayed, he looked like the corpse in Weegee's 1939 photograph, "Crime Scene of David 'the Beetle' Beadle." You're only as good as your last fight. Or your last photo. Weegee said it himself: "One day you're a hero, the next day you're a bum."

CHAPTER NINETEEN: THE FORMULA FOR FAILURE

On the flight home from Miami, Quinny didn't talk to anyone for hours. Nobody even looked at him. He had a face like the fucking Elephant Man.

Bartley sat in stunned silence; his lip occasionally quivered like he was fighting to hold back tears. Quinny felt like he let his father down and broke his heart, but he spent a lifetime letting that man down; this had to be something worse.

If Quinny had the self-confidence and the access to a weapon, he would have eaten a gun. He reckoned he'd probably fuck that up too, like one of those people who attempt to Cobain themselves and fail. He'd end up a vegetable with an underpaid nurse wiping his ass for the rest of his miserable days.

Quinny turned to his father. "It's all gone, isn't it?"

"That's how much I believed in you, son," Bartley said.

"Bullshit. You're just a degenerate gambler. You can't help yourself."

Bartley put the palms of his hands over his face and let out a sigh.

"How much?" Quinny asked.

"Everything."

"My end too?"

Bartley nodded yes.

The entire fight purse was gone before Quinny could even drown his sorrows in a beer.

The final indignity? Knowing he took that beating for nothing. Greaser Jack got half of the fight purse for putting it together, and he got Quinny's half for taking Bartley's bet. Quinny couldn't even call himself a prize fighter because there was never any prize.

Jimmy Quinn was not okay.

Somewhere over Maryland or Virginia, he had a haunting thought he couldn't shake: *Maybe I'm not actually a good fighter. Maybe I never was.*

Sure, he could kick ass against weak burnout kids at CBGB matinees and knock out drunks at bars. He could beat the shit out of untrained convicts. That's because his dad put gloves on him at four years old. Bartley wanted Quinny to be the first white American heavyweight champion since Marciano. That's what kept him going. He hauled shit for a living so his son could fulfill his dream.

He realized the old guy held out hope until the very end. Somewhere in that thick skull of his, he really believed that his thirty-eight-year-old son, who'd never fought professionally, and only fought a real opponent once—and that was a near disaster—could beat a champion fighter. That's not even taking into consideration the state of his boy's Padre Pio hand.

Quinny gave himself a five percent chance of winning the Kashan fight. Maybe Roman would gas out. Maybe he'd walk into something. Maybe his chin really was cracked. But his dad was one hundred percent certain he was going to outbox that guy with the Crazy Monkey defense he learned a couple of weeks before the fight.

Madness.

Quinny landed in New York and took an illegal cab back to his room at the motel. There was a young guy behind the desk instead of Myrna. The new guy summoned Quinny over.

"Mr. Quinn," he said, "welcome back. I have some difficult news. Your role here has been reduced." He fixed his gaze just over Quinny's shoulder to avoid eye contact.

"Reduced?"

"You're no longer needed on premises. We would appreciate you vacating your room by tomorrow morning."

"You're shitcanning me?"

"Me? "No, this wasn't my decision," he said, "but it's a clear case of overcompensation. If we need on-site security, we can pay someone ten dollars an hour whilst monetizing the room you've been occupying. Better financial outcome for investors."

Quinny was taken aback when he heard "whilst." *This had to be the first-ever usage of that pretentious word in the borough of Brooklyn.* Quinny moved in closer to make the robotic guy uncomfortable. He stood his ground. In fact, Quinny was surprised to see the guy's complete lack of personal space awareness. *If anybody stood this close to me, I'd bash their face in.*

"Yeah. Still, I had a gentleman's agreement with Jakub," Quinny said. "I like your style. All business. But if I'm gonna get axed, Jakub's gotta be the one to swing it."

"Jakub's been promoted within the company," he said. "He's the new VP of Hospitality. This motel is no longer his responsibility—it's mine. You must vacate your room and your position."

Quinny was too dejected to break his face for talking to him like a man who'd never been punched in the mouth for something he said. It was bad enough that he was a now-homeless loser, he didn't need to sink deeper into the abyss because he couldn't cope with losing his no-show job.

"Things change fast for you when you're down," Quinny said to no one.

It wasn't a family-owned motel. It was one of dozens in the portfolio of a giant company. Quinny didn't take it personally. If he had won the fight, he knew he'd still be working there. Maybe even promoted to manager. He'd be greeting and gladhanding guests. Nobody wanted a loser around. It felt contagious.

All in all, Jakub was a nice guy for looking out for him when Quinny needed a place to stay, and he needed a tough guy to stand next to. It was a mutually beneficial relationship while it lasted. Let's be honest—who wants a motel bouncer with one eye swollen shut, a cracked orbital bone, and a nose that goes horizontally instead of vertically?

Getting beat up in such a public manner was life changing. Quinny's entire identity used to be defined by a crime he committed when he was eighteen. Now he was known as the guy who took a public beating twenty years later.

Quinny strolled toward Quinn and Son Scrap Metal lost in his thoughts.

He was retired from the sport now. *Who would pay a nickel to watch me fight again?* For the first time, Quinny didn't know who he was. He wasn't a fighter. He wasn't an inmate. He wasn't a Graveyard Stomper. He wasn't a hardcore kid. He didn't have a job. He didn't even have a home anymore. He was nobody. He was nothing.

He didn't have friends. Tommy was loyal because Quinny bullied his bullies for him back in the day, but gratitude wasn't friendship. Tommy was dead. Quinny caught himself hoping his father would hire him as a helper when his hands healed up. His one and only job prospect. It made him feel sick. *Imagine being famous with no way to parlay that into making a living.*

Quinny made it to the scrap yard. He chewed the last two Oxy pills in the bottle and opened the passenger side door of his father's Dodge Ram. He sat in the front seat, grabbed the keys from the driver's seat visor, and turned the car on. He sat in dread waiting for the old guy to come back. It was a humid night. He hoped his father would run the air conditioner. The truck had a tape player, which was cool because Bartley kept all his son's old tapes, and he got to listen to them again after all this time. He put in Killing Time's "Brightside" album. The song "Backtrack" came on. Quinny turned the volume all the way up and screamed along to the hardcore classic. *One step forward, one step forward, one step forward, two steps back.*

Bartley shuffled through gravel toward his truck. He hunched over and walked like he was eighty years old. He was only fifty-seven. He was probably dying and didn't know it or preferred not to tell anyone. Or maybe he was just drunk. He slowly made his way into the driver's seat, gingerly propelling his body up the high step and into the truck. He yelled at Quinny about the music. Quinny got lost in the lyrics to the song. His dad ejected the tape and put on the AM radio sports talk.

"Dad," Quinny said, "was it all bullshit?"

"Was what bullshit?"

"Did Tyrus Raymond take a dive?"

Bartley didn't answer, but his body language was enough of an answer for Quinny. He didn't look distraught or angry at such a suggestion. That meant yes.

"And the Bullhammer? I've seen thousands of fights, and I've never seen that punch land except in my fight against Tyrus Raymond. You gassed me up."

"You gonna cry about Santa Claus not being real too?" Bartley said. "Jesus Christ." He turned forty-five degrees toward Quinny. "You were always a tough kid. You always had massive power, but you were afraid to use it. You doubted yourself. Boxers can't do that. You can't go out there thinking the other guy is better than you. So, I gave you the Bullhammer. It's Dumbo's fucking feather. It was a way to give you some confidence, all right."

The old guy looked relieved, like he was finally unburdened by a heavy secret. Quinny's bandaged hands shook. He looked away from his father and out the window, taking in the squalid junkyard. "I'm not a fighter, I'm just a wannabe."

"Jimmy," Bartley said. He never called his boy Jimmy. "Don't think about things like that. Why don't you take the back seat and get some proper sleep tonight? I'll turn the air all the way up for you."

"I'm good in the front seat" he said, "but you're not gonna be able to sleep without a blanket if the air is on."

"It's okay, Jimmy; I'll be fine."

"No," he said, "I know how you hate air conditioning. I'm gonna get you a blanket."

"It's not so easy," Bartley said. "Gotta go to the twenty-four-hour laundromat on Flatbush. Nobody uses clotheslines anymore. They haven't in thirty years."

"Dad," Quinny said, "let me do this for you."

Quinny walked off and wandered in the night. He arrived at the old house he lived in with his parents. The new owners had installed a driveway leading to the backyard. He walked the length of it in silence, making his way to the utility pole. There was no overgrown grass or short fence to boost himself up on. He leapt and grabbed a hold of the lineman's spike, performing a chin-up that opened his palm wound to get an aerial view of the clotheslines of Avenue P. His father was right—no one hung their clothes out anymore.

There was a wooden doghouse in Frankie the Screw's yard. There had to be a blanket for the dog in there. Out of pure instinct, Quinny climbed the Screw's fence. He gingerly attempted to make his way up the fence, but his heavyweight bulk caused him to pull the rusted-out slats and chain links down, making an awful racket.

He wasn't twelve years old anymore. He walked toward the doghouse with purpose and dropped to his hands and knees in front of it, rummaging around in search of a blanket. He pulled out a dog's bed and felt the cold metal of Frankie's gun against the back of his head. Quinny kept his head flush against the gun barrel and rotated his body until he was facing an elderly Frankie the Screw. As Frankie cocked the hammer, Quinny smiled and said, "Fuck you, old man, you'd be doing me a favor."

END

ACKNOWLEDGMENTS

All the love and respect in the world to Meirav Devash for putting up with me while I was writing and obsessing over this thing.

Massive thanks to Tim and Steph Murr for believing in my ability to tell a story, and to Heather Buckley for hooking me up with St. Rooster Books. Chris Rhatigan and Matthew Louis, your edits were invaluable.

Shout out to Xochitl Gonzalez, Todd Robinson, Rob Hart, and Scott Cheshire for inspiring me with your words. I'm very grateful for members of my writers' group—Greg "Jaw" Bornstein, Peter Moore Smith and Brigette Roth-Smith, Doug Donaldson, Sue Montgomery, Chris Gray and Elizabeth Stein Gray, Michael Mullen, Alice Shechter, and Gregg "The Dutchman" Van Vranken—for your guidance and kindness with the early drafts.

I'd like to acknowledge these Brooklyn legends: Frank "Ferg" Thompson, Chris Biancardi, Brian Schenk, Joe Limandri, Tim Florio, Peter Florio, Eddie Florio, Vic Christopher, Vince Maffei, Ricky Viola, Donald Currey, Marc Cianci, Pete LaRussa, Anthony Vrettos, Frank Verderame, Chris Coughlin, Jimmy McCormick, Justin Brannan, Jerry Farley, Mike Scondotto, Mark Scondotto, Jon Scondotto, Yelena Gitlin Nesbit, Tricia McCormick, Mary McNamara, Melissa Bertoncini,

James Fitzsimmons, John Blackford, Brian Lumauig, Pat Malone, Austin Collins, Frank DeAngelis, Costa Mikalakis and Bianca Sunshine, Roger Levine (RIP). Thank you to every indie record label that came out of a flyer-papered bedroom, every DIY show promoter, every hardcore band who ever played, every kid who caught a bloody nose at a Sunday matinee, every scene girl who taught her boyfriend everything he knows, every 'zine kid, tape trader, photographer, and punk pen pal.

MEET THE AUTHOR

Brooklyn Hardcore is the debut novella from Eddie McNamara, a writer from Brooklyn before it was cool. He has published short stories in *ThugLit, Shotgun Honey, J. Journal*, and others. Previously, he was a 9/11 responder, a *Penthouse* columnist, a mental health advocate, chef, and author of *Toss Your Own Salad*, a vegetarian cookbook.

ALSO FROM ST ROOSTER BOOKS

From Tim Murr

The Gray Man
978-1799252177

Lose This Skin: Collected Short Works 1994-2011
978-1530351633

Conspiracy of Birds/Hounds of Doom
978-1516920631

City Long Suffering
978-1519588074

Motel on Fire; Stories
978-1543039016

Neon Sabbath; Stories
978-1721039708

My Skull is Full of Black Smoke: Stories
979-8680276099

Thirsty and Miserable: A Critical Analysis of the Music of Black Flag
979-8609363220

Texas is the Reason: Five Decades of the Texas Chainsaw Massacre
979-8374744392

Summer's Venomous Kiss
979-8378167012

Collection/Various Authors

To Be One with You: An Anthology of Parasitic Horror 2018 featuring Paul Kane, Marie

O'Regan, Jeffery X Martin, Peter Oliver Wonder, Adam Millard, DJ Tyrer, David W Barbee, Ross Peterson

978-1724516787

Kids of the Black Hole; A Punksploitation Anthology featuring Sarah Miner, Chris Hallock, Paul Lubaczewski, and Jeremy Lowe

978-1072962724

The Blind Dead Ride Out of Hell; A Literary Tribute to the Amando de Ossorio Films featuring Sam Richard, Heather Drain, Paul Lubaczewski, Mark Zirbel, Jeremy Lowe, and Jerome Reuter

979-8692365187

A New Life by Paul Lubaczewski

979-8615384066

Blood & Mud by John Baltisberger

The God Provides by Thomas R Clark

979-8520227076

3 Hits from the Holler by Paul Lubaczewski

979-8707581984

Abhorrent Siren by John Baltisberger

978-1955745024

Let the World Drown: An Anthology of Sea Horror featuring Brian M Sammons, Lee Franklin, Jedediah Smith, AK McCarthy, Anthony S Buoni, BE Goose, Paul Lubaczewski, Jeremy Lowe, John Baltisberger, and Carter Johnson

979-8739852915

Souls in a Blender by Lamont A Turner

979-8494735201

Hungry Cosmos by Reed Alexander

979-8776862472

Black Friday: An Elder's Keep Collection by Jeffery X Martin

978-1955745093

Abhorrent Faith by John Baltisberger

978-1955745093

Short Stories About You by Jeffery X Martin

9798438145318

I Never Eat...Cheesesteak by Paul Lubaczewski

979-8440821415

Hunting Witches by Jeffery X Martin

979-8832793955

Saint's Blood by Ryan C Bradley

979-8804031863

As the Night Devours Us by Villimey Mist

979-8834327097

Parham's Field by Jeffery X Martin

SummerHome by Thomas R Clark

979-8838185136

The Ridge by Jeffery X Martin

979-8354516568

Through the Mist and the Madness: An Analytical Thesis on the First Three Metallica Albums by Jerome Reuter

979-8354143696

Like a Ton of Bricks by Paul Lubaczewski

979-8367912081

The Flock by Jeffery X Martin

979-8365780941

A Prayer from the Dead by Thomas R Clark

979-8393890742

Wax Figures by Aaron Weese

979-8390704202

Razor Blade in the Fun-Size Candy: A Horror Comedy Anthology edited by Paul Lubaczewski featuring Jeff Strand, John Wayne Communale, Bridgette Nelson, Robert Essig, Tony Evans, John Baltisberger, Mikki Nelson-Hicks, RJ Bennetti, Christine Morgan, Damien Casey, Kyra R Torres, Kenzie Jennings, Michael Allen Rose, Nikolas P Robinson

Bleeding Out in the Rain by Lamont A Turner